Marianne

WILD ROSE RIDGE HISTORICALS

LINDA JO REED

Copyright Page

Unless otherwise indicated, all Scripture quotations are taken from the King James Version of the Bible, public domain.

ISBN for print: 979-8-9998246-1-5

ISBN for e-book: 979-8-9998246-0-8

Published and printed in the United States of America

Upheld By His Hand dba Sweet Mock Orange Press

Spokane, Washington

https://www.lindajoreed.com/

Edited by Dori Harrell, Breakout Editing.

Cover design by Erin Dameron-Hill, EDH Professionals.

Map design by Heather Wilbur.

Other Books by Linda Jo Reed

Nonfiction

Upheld in the Battle

Mrs. Job's Choice

Through the Eyes of Amos

Fiction

Wild Rose Ridge Seasons Series

Cruising Claire's Dream

Kellie's Christmas Box

Kevin's Camp Surprise

Kyle's Autumn Blaze

Karen's Secret Admirer, A Wild Rose Ridge Valentine

Wild Rose Ridge Historicals

Marianne

Dedication

Friendships developed by women have always been mysterious and beautiful. Forged by the Spirit of God, I believe. That is how I view the lifelong relationships of our Wild Rose Ridge Mail Order Brides. Coming together across the nation to forge new lives and doing it together. I have lived life alongside five women whom I consider my sisters. While we didn't traverse the continent, we forged a bond through the Holy Spirit one night at a retreat. We call ourselves the Tea Counsel, since we started doing tea parties. We have counseled and prayed with one another for over thirty-five years, and now into eternity.

I dedicate this story to Sandy Alderson, Charlotte Matthews, Marcia Anderson, Arlie Robinson, and Mary Johnson. Arlie and Mary, dear ones, are sitting at the feet of Jesus in heaven. I am sure they are eagerly awaiting the arrival of the rest of us when there will be great rejoicing (and maybe heavenly tea) with our wonderful Savior.

Oh what a day that will be!

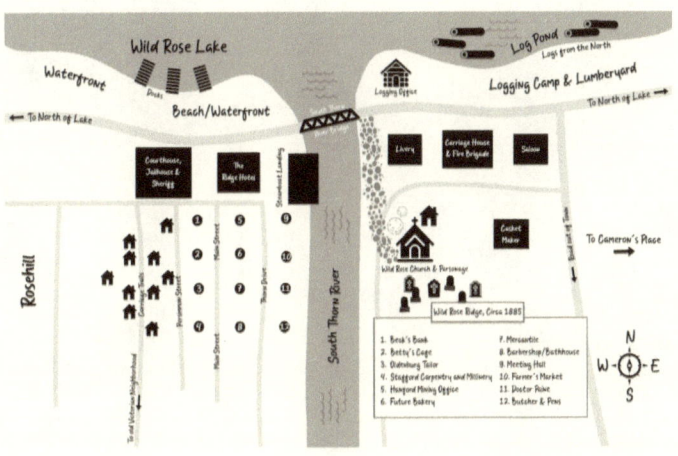

Wild Rose Lake

Waterfront

Beach/Waterfront

Log Pond

Logs from the North

Logging Camp & Lumberyard

← To North of Lake

To North of Lake →

Logging Office

Courthouse, Jailhouse & Sheriff

The Ridge Hotel

Steamboat Landing

Livery

Carriage House & Fire Brigade

Saloon

Casket Maker

To Cameron's Place →

Rosehill

Wild Rose Church & Parsonage

Wild Rose Ridge, Circa 1885

1. Beck's Bank
2. Betty's Cage
3. Oldenburg Tailor
4. Stagyard Carpentry and Millinery
5. Hungard Mining Office
6. Future Bakery

7. Mercantile
8. Barbershop/Bathhouse
9. Meeting Hall
10. Farmer's Market
11. Doctor Polke
12. Butcher & Pens

South Thorn River

N
W · E
S

Prologue

December 12, 1885
   Wild Rose Ridge
   Dearest Mama,

   I hope this missive finds you and your husband well.

   We arrive today in Wild Rose Ridge in Washington Territory. It has been a long, arduous journey by rail and steamboat, particularly at this time of year. It is cold, but not more so than at home. And the sun is shining. It must be a good omen as we steam up the South Thorn River to the town that sits on Wild Rose Lake. I have heard the lake and the area are beautiful. I can hardly wait to see it. I look forward to spring. My new friend Meg Ennis tells me that the wild roses on the brown hills are beautiful when in bloom.

   Meg is not a bride. She has been visiting her sister in Portland and will return home to a town somewhere east of Wild Rose Ridge. Her brother will be escorting her home. I think we will be friends going forward.

   All of us mail order brides are a bit nervous. What will we find when we get there? After the *Merry Jo* docks and we've had a short rest, there is a tea reception. That is where we will meet our future husbands. I tremble even as I write these words because my future is at hand.

Elinore Cantrell and I have made friends. Her intended is a gentleman farmer. My intended has a carpentry business in town. Have I told you that he has already built a shop for me next to his? I have the trunk with enough materials to get started, at least, and thank you for insisting that I bring along a Montgomery Ward catalog. It may come in quite handy.

I am taking advantage of this time to send you my news so you may be at peace, knowing I am safe and about to begin the new life we planned. I plan to hand this letter to the purser before disembarking the Merry Jo. He will take it with her as she steams away tomorrow.

I must hurry. I hear sounds outside my cabin that tell me we are soon arriving. I admit to some anxiety. I do hope the man whose letter I possess is tall, broad, and as handsome as his photograph showed. His name is Jeremy Stafford, if I have not told you before.

I must go now, Mama. Take care of yourself. Give my regards to your husband.

Have a very happy Christmas.

Love from your daughter,

Marianne Foster.

One

"I don't think I have ever seen a more disgusting display." Marianne Foster stood at the window of her room in The Ridge Hotel in Wild Rose Ridge, gazing out at the pulsing waves of male humanity. "Just look at them! Brawling, pushing and shoving. And how they behaved when we disembarked from the *Merry Jo* is just revolting. I think I agree with Elinore when she said this was a primitive village."

Meg Ennis sat on one of the twin beds and folded her hands in her lap to regard Marianne. "It's not like this normally. My brother Samuel says the men came from miles around to get a glimpse of the mail order brides. Some businesses even closed down for the day."

Marianne snorted. She didn't care if it was an unladylike noise to make. It surely fit what she observed this day. "How are we supposed to marry men like this?"

"But not all men are so unruly."

Marianne cut her off. "Unruly? Really, Meg. They tried to grab us even as we disembarked from the boat, and they shouted marriage proposals. I'm not sure marriage is what they had in mind either."

"Not all of them acted so badly. What about the intended bridegrooms who came alongside you and protected you right into the hotel? I seem to recall a nice gentleman walking with you."

"One would think you a bride by the way you defend them." Marianne sat on her own bed to face her new friend.

Meg laughed. "No, not I. Samuel is here to take me home tomorrow after church. I am very ready to go home, although I think maybe we should have delayed my trip home another week so I wouldn't miss all this hullabaloo."

"I am glad we have met, Meg."

"Me too. We will write to keep in touch, and when Samuel comes into Wild Rose Ridge on occasion, I will see if I can come with him. I would like to see Elinore too."

"Yes, please. I'm sure Elinore would be happy to see you too. Oh, Meg. He's . . . he's *short*. What's more, he . . . he has a walking stick and he limps. Did you see him swing his stick?"

"Maybe to protect you?" Meg didn't ask who.

Marianne squirmed on the chair she had dropped onto, picked up her gray muff, picked at the fur, then set it down again. "He's just not what I expected." She jumped up and paced. She felt Meg's eyes follow her and worried that she had shocked her friend.

"I have to meet with him in just a few minutes and I'm supposed to be resting. How can I rest?"

"What did you expect?"

Marianne stood again at the window, moving a lace curtain just slightly. The mob of men finally seemed to be dissipating. Thank goodness. Who knew what they might have tried to do if they'd kept up that frenetic activity? She sighed and turned back to Meg.

"I don't know. I suppose I thought him taller. But I look him eye to eye. Shouldn't a man be taller than his intended?"

Meg chuckled. "You're worried about his height?"

Marianne flushed. "Well, maybe a little. His mustache looks the same as the photograph he sent. But, well, I expected to look up to him."

"A man's height does not denote his character," Meg said softly, and hesitated.

"Of course not. Do you know something about him?" Marianne paused in her pacing to stare at the other woman.

Meg picked up a book that she had been reading on the trip to Wild Rose Ridge and set it beside her. "Not much. Just that a couple years ago a logging accident killed a man, and Mr. Stafford dove in to save him and got caught in the accident himself. Everyone in the area knew about it, and Mr. Stafford has had a long convalescence."

Marianne stared out the window again. That certainly explained the stick and his limp. "Then he's some kind of hero?"

"I don't know much more than that. You already know he has built a carpentry business."

"He's brown all over," Marianne muttered.

"Brown?"

"His hair, his mustache, the clothes he wore when we crossed the boardwalk from the *Merry Jo*." She didn't need to add her impression of his striking, fine hazel eyes.

"Brown is not good?" Meg looked puzzled. "I have brown hair. You have dark hair. What's wrong with it?"

"Nothing is wrong with brown hair." Marianne moved to the dresser and picked up her brush with exasperation.

5

How could she get across feelings she wasn't sure she understood herself? She stared at the blue eyes in the mirror as she set errant dark strands of hair back into her neat bun. She fluffed the sides just a bit. "I think if he had worn another color, it would be different."

"So he is short and brown. You will have to see if he has any conversation." Meg placed the book aside. "It's nearly time for you to head downstairs for the tea. I hope you can relax and have a good talk with Mr. Stafford."

Marianne dropped the brush back onto the bureau, fixed her black feathered hat into place, and secured it with a hatpin. Mama said a lady always wore her hat. It "finished" her. Marianne then shook the skirt of her black-striped forest-green traveling dress. It wouldn't do to present herself at this interview with wrinkles.

She met Meg's brown eyes and nearly giggled. "You have very fine eyes."

"What?" Meg's face wrinkled in confusion. "What do my eyes have to do with anything?"

"They are brown." Both ladies laughed.

"Yes, I am a brown girl. You see, brown is nice."

"All right." Marianne wiped her eyes. "It's like this. I liked his letter. I thought a match might be possible, until I met him and—and then he's short. He's more slender than broad. He's just not what I envisioned. But he sent a very nice letter, so I will give him a chance."

Meg rose from the chair and crossed the room to hug Marianne.

"It's an emotional time for you. I am sure that the mail order bride idea seemed a good one until it became real. Maybe he looks all short and brown to you, but you already know that it is what is inside that is important. Will he be faithful? Will he care for you? And you don't know yet."

Marianne nodded, and her voice was muffled. "I may want to propose a partnership instead of a marriage. He's already set my shop up."

Meg backed up to the bed and plopped onto it. "Well then, you know one thing."

"What?"

"He will consider your wants and needs."

* * *

When Marianne descended the staircase, she was met at the bottom with a bevy of matronly ladies as well as Miss Valentine O'Malley. Amusement overran Marianne's anxiety for a moment. No one ever called Miss O'Malley by her given name. She corrected that swiftly. She would be known as Val—or else.

As Val separated herself from the matrons to greet and guide Marianne, the matrons followed her.

"Introduce us, please, Miss O'Malley. We need to know our brides," one of the buxom ladies insisted. "I'm Mrs. Beck. We are delighted that you are all here."

Marianne noticed her hat tipping precariously on her head. Marianne's hands itched to reposition it and push the hatpin in more securely.

"This is Miss Marianne Foster." Val moved close, as though to guard her.

Now Marianne had to fight a laugh. Val was fierce, and she came in a small package. Barely five feet tall, if that, her glossy dark hair shown under her tastefully small hat. Val had shepherded her flock safely from Chicago, and it seemed she intended to continue her vigilance.

"Oh, you are lovely, my dear. Let's see, we have you paired with Mr. Jeremy Stafford. Is that right?" Another lady checked a paper she carried and peered at Marianne. This lady's hat was set on her head at a fashionable angle. "And you are a milliner, am I correct?"

Before Marianne could respond, Val said, "This is Mrs. Schulte, Marianne." She turned to the lady. "Yes, she will be setting up a millinery business."

A third matron pushed forward. She was decked out in jewelry and had several rings on her gloved fingers. She held out a hand to Marianne, who wondered if she should curtsey or kiss the hand.

"I am Mrs. Hanford. So pleased you all arrived safely."

Marianne touched the woman's fingers, and Mrs. Hanford drew her hand away. Phew.

"Now, ladies, if you will excuse us, I will escort Marianne to Mr. Stafford." Val slipped her arm through Marianne's and led her away.

"That's another one down," Val muttered.

"Who are they?" Marianne whispered. "I'm in awe of them."

"They call themselves the Busy Bees. They seem to run the town. I'm not sure, but I think the men around here are afraid of them."

Both women giggled.

"They have met each bride before I escorted them to their intendeds. It's a strange ritual. But these ladies brought us here to tame their town, I think. And to establish some kind of society, I'm sure. Ah, here is Mr. Stafford. I see tea has been delivered to your table. It's so nice to meet you, sir. This is Miss Marianne Foster. I shall leave you to it." Val disengaged her arm from Marianne's after a gentle, encouraging squeeze.

Val left, and Marianne was faced with the man before her. They stood eye to eye, and that still startled her. Why was she so concerned with how tall he was? She kept her gaze trained on his face. Hazel. His eyes were hazel. Green, flecked with golden brown. Like the sun glancing off a velvet-brown hill in the distance.

She shook her head slightly. Where did that thought come from?

"Miss Foster, welcome to Wild Rose Ridge. I've looked forward to your arrival." She stood frozen as he bowed, his eyes on hers.

"T-Thank you. Mr. Stafford."

He straightened with a smile and stepped back, unhurried. She relaxed.

"I hope your journey wasn't too exhausting." Still smiling, he held out a chair for her. He leisurely moved around the table to sit in the chair opposite her.

Was he a deliberate kind of person who took his time in movements? Or perhaps that was due to his injury. She discreetly looked around for his walking stick and saw it leaning against the wall.

"Not at all." She shook her head. "The vastness of our country is remarkable. And the landscape changes are immense. We saw buffalo herds. What grand creatures."

"Yes, they are. I admit that I am partial to this territory. A land offering many opportunities."

His eyes stayed on her, and his smile never wavered, and she managed a smile in return. He was still short. She'd hoped for a tall, brawny man. But he was neat, in spite of his brown attire, and a hint of pine wafted from him—or was that the pine boughs that decorated the room for Christmas?

Red velvet roses covered the walls, and beautifully crafted wall sconces held lit wicks inside glass bulbs. Pine boughs with festive red ribbons woven through them flowed across the walls and adorned a fireplace with a blazing fire. A lovely room that greeted hotel visitors. She wondered if they had many.

"Would you do the honors?"

Marianne's attention jerked back to Mr. Stafford. He indicated the teapot.

"Oh yes, of course." She poured tea into their cups, and he subtly pushed the finger sandwiches toward her. He had manners. That was in his favor. But she wasn't sure she could eat, since her stomach was knotted up.

"It's much better to see you than to decipher words on a page, don't you think?"

"Yes, I agree." Settling her cup back in its saucer, Marianne swept an arm around to indicate the room. "You said in your letter that you are a carpenter. Did you make some of the furnishings in this room?"

He looked around. "Yes, I carved the wall sconces and had a hand in making the cabinets and buffets that hold the dishes you see around the room, as well as some of the other pieces. Thank you for noticing."

"Everything is nicely elegant, Mr. Stafford." She could almost see him grow taller with the praise.

"Please, call me Jeremy."

She hesitated. She should give him permission to use her given name as well. But she didn't know him. Yet he was her intended. My, what a thought.

"And I am Marianne." There, she said it.

He smiled again, and his handsome eyes lit up. Yes, even if he was short, she could admit to his striking eyes that could surely hold the attention of any woman. A rush of warmth slid into her heart.

"Marianne. A beautiful name."

She would have thanked him for the compliment, but he continued to speak.

"You said in your letter that you have siblings who have settled here in the West. Whereabouts are they, if I may ask?"

"Of course you may ask. I did mention them. Mostly my brothers brought their families out West. They are much older than I and came with the wagon trains. Two went to California, and one is in the Oregon country. My sister married and stayed close to Mama back East. Mama remarried and still lives there. It was time for me to seek my own future." Her words came out in a rush. That was enough to reveal, all Jeremy would need to know. "You said, in your letter, that you are a younger sibling as well?"

"Yes, I am a younger son. I understand the urge to make your own way in the world. My Pa was lost in the War Between the States. My eldest brother has run the store since I can remember, and Mother lives with his family. The rest of us are scattered, as yours are."

"I'm sorry about your father."

That smile again. "Thank you. It was so long ago. I don't remember him much."

"Then you came here."

"I did. I worked in the logging camp at the north end of Wild Rose Lake for a few years. Then I came to town and established a carpentry business."

"You must love your work."

"I do. I hope you will let me escort you through town. I am eager to show you my carpentry shop, but mostly your own shop. I tried to fashion it the way you envisioned it from your letter."

What was he saying?

Too much, too soon.

11

"Oh yes, of course." Marianne pulled her scattered thoughts together. "Thank you for such consideration. I am looking forward to opening my business."

His smile slipped a little. "I hope it meets with your expectations."

Oh dear. She took a deep breath. Was this going to work? He seemed nice, but, talking about expectations, he wasn't what she'd imagined him to be. Yet, what exactly did she expect? And what was too fast when one was a mail order bride? And she did write to him about her plans to open a millinery shop. She just had not expected him to build it before she arrived.

She intended to approach her plan for partnership. Quickly.

"You are most kind, Jeremy. For anticipating my hopes for my shop. And for making it possible for me to come."

His smile widened.

A door opened noisily, and a man and a young girl breezed into the room. Marianne saw Val hurry over to Ella, a friend to one of the brides, as the man approached her. For a moment, Marianne was distracted, wondering why he'd approached Ella. Then she returned her attention to Jeremy.

She avoided looking into those beautiful eyes and straightened her back. Taking a deep breath, she spoke. "Can we talk? I have a proposition."

* * *

Jeremy Stafford couldn't help the smile that beamed from his face. He had a chance at a new life. A future to work for. A legacy.

His bride was beautiful. They would have a beautiful life. Her name sounded beautiful.

Marianne.

Wait. What did she say?

Jeremy stared. What did she mean—a proposition?

He waited. She fidgeted. He waited some more.

She took two deep breaths. Ran her fingers along the table. Then she looked at him.

"I've been thinking a lot. Especially the closer we came to Wild Rose Ridge."

Waiting seemed to be the order of the day for him. What was coming?

"And . . . and I think we should wait on marriage."

Even though he somehow expected that, a jolt shot through him anyway. He barely maintained his poise, when he wanted to slam back against his chair with angry surprise.

"Why?"

"We don't know each other. And . . . and I thought maybe we could do a business partnership instead." She fixed her eyes on the drama happening in another corner of the room.

"Instead?"

"Y-yes. You have put so much thought and work into my shop. I can't thank you enough. I thought perhaps you might agree to my renting the shop from you. As my business grows, I can pay you back for all the expenses."

A silence fell.

Of course, shattered dreams didn't make noise, but Jeremy felt the shards falling all around him. His plans for a wife, family, and a legacy dropped at his feet.

Legacy would evade him.

Had he done something wrong? Been too eager? Scared

13

her away? All he had done was with her comfort in mind. How could she deceive him? Had she planned this from the beginning, never intending to actually be a bride?

"Is it because I am a cripple?" He asked harshly as the last reason surfaced. The one he most dreaded. What else could it be?

"No, of course not," she denied.

He watched her. She briefly glanced at him, then looked away. She picked up her teacup and set it down again, without a sip. All right, she was nervous. It took courage to broach this change of plan after letters, travel, and even the money that exchanged hands.

"No."

She looked up and opened her mouth, but he held up his hand and sat straight.

"I need a wife. I bought a wife. I will have a wife. You signed a contract. You came on the pretext of being a mail order bride. I plan for us to wed immediately, and then you can set up shop."

Two

"Insufferable man!"

Meg, sitting at the window, nearly dropped the darning dowel over which she was repairing a stocking. "Good gracious. What happened?"

Marianne stormed to her bed, threw her hat on it, and shoved her muff aside. She flopped onto it and jumped up again. Her hands resting on her hips, she swung around.

"He's trying to force me to marry him."

Meg's eyebrows rose.

"Yes he is." Marianne paced back and forth.

Meg watched Marianne's jerky steps for a minute, then returned to her darning.

"Yes, yes, I know. That is what I came to do in the first place. But how can I marry a stranger? He refused to even reflect on my proposal to be partners instead of married. I laid it out concisely. I explained how I would pay him back as my business grew. You know what he said?" Marianne stopped in front of Meg with her arms held out.

"What did he say?"

Marianne scrunched up her face and lowered her voice. "'I need a wife. I bought a wife, and I will have a wife.'"

Meg looked up. "He didn't."

"He did."

"Then what happened?" Meg's eyes rounded.

"I excused myself and came up here. How does he think I can come and step off a boat and straight into a marriage? I couldn't discuss it. I just saw red. I could hardly countenance his arrogance. 'I will have a wife' indeed!"

"What will you do now?"

Her anger spent, Marianne's shoulders drooped, and she sank onto the bed. She picked up the abused hat and smoothed the feathers around the crown before setting it gently onto the small table next to the bed. "I don't know, Meg." Marianne wandered to the window. "The *Merry Jo* leaves tomorrow."

"They have been loading all afternoon."

Marianne felt Meg's sharp gaze on her back. But she had to ask. "Did anyone board her again?"

"Yes. I think one of the brides left. I gather she didn't think too much of the place or her man. Does it matter? Are you considering leaving?"

"No, of course not." Marianne sat on the bed. Now that she had calmed somewhat, she reflected that she really did sign a contract, and a man had paid her way with a purpose in sight. What had she been thinking? She sighed. Thinking that she was not welcome in the home she had grown up in. She had to make her way in the world, and there were not a lot of options for a woman alone. She twisted her hands in her lap.

"Maybe you should consult Miss O'Malley about your doubts. Dealing with bride issues is what she is here to do, isn't it?"

"Yes, you're right. I'll go look for her now." Marianne rose from the bed. As she crossed the room, a knock came from the door.

Marianne swung it open to find Val O'Malley on the other side. Her shiny black hair was piled on her head, which added a little more to her barely five-foot frame. Relief flooded Marianne. Val had been a champion for more than one of them at times. She packed a punch. Marianne could use some of that right now.

"Oh." Val's hand was raised for another knock, and she dropped it to her side. "Just who I want to see. I saw you leave the tea. And we must meet soon with the Busy Bees concerning your wedding details. They have set it for tomorrow right after church. What is wrong?"

Val scrutinized her. Marianne put a hand to her throat. Had she known the wedding would be tomorrow? Could Val see clear to the back of Marianne's head and discern her thoughts?

"I . . . I'm having second thoughts, I think. Tomorrow?" Could she make more sense?

"Let's chat. Is your room all right?"

"Yes, Meg knows."

Val slipped an arm around Marianne and came into the room, closing the door behind her.

"I'll leave." Meg set aside her dowel and rose from the chair.

"You don't have to," Marianne began.

"I want to be downstairs when my brother arrives. He'll be hungry and ready for dinner, so I'll make those arrangements now." Meg bustled out the door.

Marianne sat on her bed again, and Val took the vacated chair. Marianne wasn't usually so indecisive, but now she felt like her nerve endings were waving in the air, little ends stinging. She shook her head. She had always prided herself on her practicality, not fanciful imaginings.

Was it practical to be a mail order bride? It must be—what were the alternatives? She could not return home.

"What is bothering you, Marianne?"

"I hardly know," Marianne admitted. "I thought I had everything settled in my mind. But now that reality has manifested, I hardly know what I am doing."

"Was Mr. Stafford unpleasant? Is there anything about him that feels threatening?"

"No, oh no, not at all." She gave Val an accounting of the discussion with Mr. Stafford.

"Everything was quite cordial until I broached the subject of partnership. When I offered my plan of partnership, rather than marriage, he said he needed a wife, bought a wife, and would have a wife." Marianne huffed. "He reminded me that I had signed a contract to marry him. He seemed so much more the gentleman in his letters. I don't know this man."

Val looked out the window, a half smile on her lips. After a moment, she fixed her gaze on Marianne. "None of you know the men you agreed to come and marry. Perhaps putting your trust in God will help you have peace in your heart. Mr. Stafford seems like a nice man to me. He has a steady business, and he built a shop for you." Val's calm manner settled into Marianne's spirit. "Is there any specific objection you have to Mr. Stafford?"

"I asked myself that same question, even while he was telling me how he had built my shop already. He was kind, even eager to please. I only saw his arrogance when we argued over partnership or marriage. Even then he was calm and controlled."

"Well then . . ." Val paused. "Could it be his lameness?"

Marianne slowly shook her head, eyeing her hands in her lap. Was it? She'd been quick to deny it when Jeremy had asked.

"That would make me a despicable person." She met Val's look. "I don't want to think so. I was already entertaining the idea of partnership before I formally met him. His injury is a surprise, but it can be overcome."

Val nodded. "I believe you. What, then, holds you back? The real reason?"

Marianne hesitated again and widened her eyes. "I think it's fear. Of the unknown."

Val nodded again. "All right, let's see if we can move beyond that. Does the motivation for coming still exist?"

"Yes. I left home when my mother remarried and my stepfather made it plain that I needed to make other arrangements for my future. A brand-new adventure seemed like a good idea." Well, this certainly was an adventure.

"We all have come to marry men who want to build families and community here in Wild Rose Ridge. I think that's a great purpose, don't you?"

"I suppose I do, or I wouldn't have come. It's just that he is not what I expected."

"Maybe he is better than you expected."

Marianne sighed. "I suppose I have nothing to be angry about. He has held up his end of the bargain, and now I see that I must as well. But, Val, he wants to be wed immediately. I-I don't think I can, well, be a wife so soon."

Val leaned over to lay her hand over Marianne's. "Is he asking you to? Or is he simply insisting on the marriage commitment for now?"

Marianne straightened her back. "Of course. I will

make that stipulation. That we must get to know each other before, ah, that."

Val stood, a twinkle in her eye. "I think more than you will be making that stipulation. Let's go see about meeting the Bees over our dinner and planning tomorrow's wedding."

* * *

The tinny sound of a faraway piano drifted in the air. The saloon, across the river, was open for business. Jeremy had spent too many Saturday nights in the past there with his buddies. He didn't miss it. But he sure could use some kind of distraction about now. Considering his bride wasn't of the same mind to marry that he was cut to the heart. He limped down the darkened street toward his shop—and hers—and home behind it, the tapping of his walking stick grating on his spirit.

He paused to stare at the stick. He had carved it himself. He wasn't sure he would have done it without Doc Paine's challenge.

It was the shaping of the stick that had given him a new direction. He had discovered his talent for woodworking, and with his friend Thad McNeil's help and encouragement, his business thrived. He stabbed the ground with the stick and took another step.

He reflected on a verse in the Bible from the book of Philippians. This verse kept him moving forward. *Being confident of this very thing, that he which hath begun a good work in you will perform it until the day of Jesus Christ.*

Confidence. That was the thing that he had lost in that logging accident. How could a man lead a productive life if his body didn't work right? Still, God gave him ideas and energy to work with wood. He had swallowed his pride and hired help when he had needed to do so. And townsfolk hired him to make furniture and facias for their buildings.

Thank you for your strength, my God. Thank you for all you have done for me. Now what would you have me do about this reluctant bride?

The arrangements were already in process; the town's Busy Bees assured him of that. The wedding was scheduled for tomorrow after church. Neither of them really had a choice but to show up.

Was he making a mistake? Had he made her hostile to him? He'd been so bowled over by her beauty. Would he have reconsidered otherwise?

No. Besides her beauty, he sensed kindness in her, even though she wanted to back out. On the other hand, it took courage for her to make the trip for this purpose as she had. Perhaps that would be a better way to look at it. She had courage.

Maybe they would both need it.

"Hey, Stafford, thought you got one of them brides? What happened? What you doing out here? She reject you?"

Jeremy squinted, trying to see who addressed him. The voice was familiar. He didn't like the idea that someone might know his business, even if it was some kind of jest. The farther he left the hotel behind, the darker the street became in spite of the streetlights. His vision narrowed in on Ambrose Kircher.

His nemesis.

"What are you doing over here, Kircher? I didn't know you had sent for a bride."

"You never know. Maybe not this time. Gotta see what's in there first. Maybe next time."

Kircher's breath wafted toward Jeremy, and he scrunched his nose. The saloon would be a better place for Kircher to be. The man veered toward the street and turned toward the river. As Jeremy watched him, Kircher's sneer was the last thing he saw as the other man rounded a corner.

Jeremy watched him disappear. What reason would Ambrose Kircher have for being in town this night?

* * *

"Are you trying to kill that chair?"

Jeremy looked up from pounding nails into a piece of furniture ordered by a customer. Since he had returned from the hotel, he had been working furiously trying to calm his inner turmoil.

He threw down the hammer and sat back on his heels, ignoring the pain in his knees. He wiped his sleeve across his forehead.

"What brings you by tonight, Thad?"

"Well, I'm due here for a wedding tomorrow. I thought I might be able to bunk here tonight. The hotel is pretty full, and I was barely able to get Ma and Amelia registered there for tonight. They want to stay a few days to shop for Christmas too. I sure didn't expect to see your light on in here tonight."

Jeremy's friend dropped a knapsack in a corner, leaned against an unfinished bureau, and crossed his arms. He apparently expected an answer.

Jeremy grunted and pulled himself up to sit on a sawhorse.

"That's all I get? A grunt? Tell me about your bride."

"You sure are blunt."

"It's a failing of mine, and you have known that for a

long time. So tell." Thad pushed back his cowboy hat to get a better look at Jeremy. "I don't know how you can see to work in this dim light. On a Saturday night is unusual enough, but maybe I should ask why you aren't courting."

"You're not going away, are you?"

"Nope."

Jeremy wiped his face again and sighed. "I made a mess of things. I couldn't wait for her to get here, and now I almost wish I'd never sent for her."

"That bad?"

Jeremy met his friend's look. Thad was like a brother. But sometimes, like now, he wished Thad was somewhere else. But Thad had been a steadfast friend during Jeremy's convalescence at Thad's farm after the logging accident that had taken Jeremy's knees out last year.

The McNeil family had welcomed Jeremy like one of their own, and Louisa McNeil had cared for him as if he were her own son until he could walk again. He'd always be grateful at how Louisa had taken him in. Now she did his upholstery for him. It was a small way to demonstrate that gratefulness. She called the compensation her "egg money."

Thad had kept Jeremy from despair and encouraged him to keep his faith and trust God for his future. He would always be grateful for Thad's help in establishing his carpentry shop.

"She's beautiful, Thad. I couldn't believe my good fortune."

Thad's eyebrows went up. "But?"

"But when we met at that blasted tea this afternoon, she talked about a partnership instead of a marriage. I said no. I wanted a wife and sent for one. And she signed a contract. She clammed up after that and excused herself. I came home."

"Whoowee! You know how to make an impression, don't you?"

"Thanks for the sympathy."

"Well, are you still intent on marrying her?"

"Yep. You know it's been set up for tomorrow since the Bees sent for the brides. Christmas is coming quick, and the town will have festivities going on. I have promised finished projects before Christmas that I need to have settled before then." Jeremy leaned over, picked up the hammer, and tapped it on the sawhorse. "So the wedding must go on as planned."

"You sure you want to do that after this first discussion with her didn't go so well?" Thad shifted and folded his arms to lean more comfortably.

"Yep. I've already got her shop ready. She just needs to decorate it and move in. But you know my plans, Thad. It's time I got a wife." Jeremy tossed the hammer up and down. "She seems like a nice lady. I like that she thinks for herself and has worked on a plan."

"Now you are backing up on almost wishing you'd never sent for her?"

Jeremy snorted. "Okay, yeah. Backing up. Still want to stand up with me?"

"Of course I will. I just told you that Ma and my sister are already here. Back to my accommodations for tonight. Can I stay here?" Thad dropped his arms and placed his hands behind him as he looked around.

"Sure. But you can't stay more than tonight." Jeremy held in his grin.

"Huh."

Now Jeremy looked around at all his unfinished projects. Could the brides have come at a worst time? How could he concentrate on making a new wife happy and still complete his projects?

"I can see your thoughts, friend. Let me help you tonight so you can spend time with your bride tomorrow tonight." Thad tossed his hat and coat on his knapsack and rolled up his sleeves. "Won't do you any good to refuse. I'm going to help anyway. I don't think either of us have anything else to do right now."

Jeremy laughed. "Thanks, buddy. All I've been doing is fuming anyway. I welcome your company."

They worked in companionable silence, hammering, sawing, and polishing. Jeremy was grateful for Thad's help. He was grateful for Thad's friendship.

He hoped tomorrow night would not be a war zone.

Three

Marianne shivered as she stopped on the bridge that spanned the South Thorn River. She took in the watery scene. Wild Rose Lake on her left drained into the river under the bridge and to her right. Rain drizzled. Everything about the lake was gray today.

The brides trudged this morning from the hotel in town to Wild Rose Community Church, which stood east side of the river. The same river they had steamed up yesterday in sunshine. The *Merry Jo* bumped against the dock. The boat would leave today with Marianne's letter to her mother. And the ex-bride.

A gust of wind and rain whipped around them.

"Whose idea was this?" She readjusted her felt bonnet. She wanted her ears covered against the cold. She reflected that she might add winter bonnets in many colors in her shop once she set it up. Surely the women here would need them.

"Look, isn't it beautiful?" Meg, who accompanied the

brides to church, stopped to shake out the soggy hem of her gown and gazed out at the lake.

"Even with the logs floating here?" Elinore asked. "That rather spoils the beauty. That is, if it is beautiful on a good weather day."

"It was yesterday," Meg responded.

"I suppose the lumber yard is necessary for business." Marianne's gaze swept from the pool of bobbing logs as the waters slurped around them to the gray skies and mist shrouding the hills that ringed the lake. What a dreary day. Which fit her mood just fine.

"I am guessing that the saloon music we heard last night is just beyond the lumber yard." Cornelia Rose, another bride, set her gloved hand on the bridge railing and snatched it back. "Oh bother! Now my glove is soaked."

"Likely it is," Marianne agreed. The tinny saloon music had kept her from sleeping late into the night. Well, that and her meeting with Jeremy Stafford. And accepting that today would be her wedding day, then worrying about her wedding clothes arriving at the church safe and dry. Marianne looked out over the lake and blinked gritty eyes several times. "I certainly hope spring brings those wild roses we've heard so much about. All I see now is fog, rain, and water."

"Don't be so gloomy. It's winter." Meg flung out an arm toward the lake. "Spring will come and the warmth with it. For now, the snow and the clouds drifting by make the scenery so ethereal, don't you think?"

"Pretty ghostly, all right."

Meg laughed. "You will need to invest in warmer clothing."

"We'd better catch up with the others, or we will be late for service." Elizabeth Ann picked up her skirt and strode off the bridge.

They hurried along, and Marianne noted the river water scrambled along the shore as the path snaked on toward the white clapboard church. The only sound was the squishing of their boots in the mud. She grimaced.

Relieved to finally arrive at the church, Marianne looked forward to drying out. Until she stepped inside, and the odor of unwashed bodies and liquor assailed her.

In church?

She nearly backed out into the rain. But with Elinore and Meg behind her, Marianne had no choice but continue into the odorous building. She wrinkled her nose.

"Makes one want to hold a kerchief to the nose, doesn't it?" Elinore whispered. Both women giggled.

A line of unkempt men with hair and beards mingling together sat at the back of the church. Their clothes were wrinkled and stained. What Marianne noticed most were the leers on their faces. Did they come straight from the saloon to the church? Had they never seen women before? How silly. They probably had seen some colorful women last night.

She pulled her thoughts away from that scenario.

She snapped her eyes forward and slipped her arm through Elinore's as they made their way up the aisle, Val marching in front of them. Meg met her brother and moved into the church with him, behind Marianne.

Closer to the front, in contrast, men stood clean and dressed neatly. Some with families. But mostly men alone, yet together.

How confusing. But this was the Wild West, right? She had better get used to it. She felt the stares burning into her back.

Unsettled, she looked over her shoulder. Once. The smelly men still leered. She even heard a burp.

A burp!

Her gaze snagged on one of those men. He wasn't leering. He was scowling. His narrowed eyes seemed to be directed at her. How could that be? She had not even been in town for twenty-four hours yet. She sat stiffly, staring at the front of the church again.

Marianne scanned the men at the front again. There. Jeremy Stafford sat on the end of an aisle watching her. He dipped his head as their eyes met. She saw kindness in his face this morning. Not anger. She let out a breath she had probably been holding since walking away from him yesterday. If this marriage was going to work, she would have to meet him halfway.

* * *

Preacher Micah Sutton had prepared a sermon to welcome the brides, and it seemed to Jeremy that he would never end this sermon extolling the virtues of marriage and the responsibilities of the men who had brought a bride to town.

The hymns were led by the Dawes sisters, who fancied themselves musicians. Jeremy groaned as yet another off-key not-so-musical note sounded from the organ. He grimaced as he waited for the inevitable voice of the other sister to warble in before the congregation started to sing. It had to be the last song, didn't it? Sometime soon?

Finally it was over, and people stood to greet one another. As if they hadn't already done so before the service. Usually they all stampeded for the door to get to their Sunday dinner roasts.

But not today.

No, today would provide a spectacle in the church.

Two weddings. One of which was his own. Jeremy looked around. The Busy Bees were already managing the setup for the ceremony. Their voices carried over one another.

Jeremy looked to the back of the church, where Miss Foster still lingered with another bride. Miss Cantrell, wasn't it? He started that direction.

A throat cleared next to him. "Are you ready for this?" Robert Cameron nodded his head once in the direction of their brides. He straightened his tie and fell into step with Jeremy, still heading toward the ladies.

"I certainly could have wished for a private ceremony without the town fanfare, that's for sure. But yes, I am ready. How about you?" Jeremy aligned his legs as he pitched his stick ahead with each leg. It wouldn't do to be limping.

"Mother and I are looking forward to Miss Cantrell coming home with us today."

"Your mother looks lovely today. I'm glad she is here," Jeremy said simply. Robert Cameron was his friend, but the town shunned his mother. Jeremy never knew why. She always treated him kindly whenever he was around her. Robert was very protective of her but had never explained the town's rejection of her, and Jeremy chose to ignore the gossip.

"Thank you."

"Good morning, Miss Foster, Miss Cantrell." Jeremy slightly bowed before them and noticed Robert did the same. He fixed his gaze on Miss Foster. "May I speak with you a moment?"

Panic flared momentarily in her eyes, and he cursed himself for causing it. Perhaps after yesterday she thought he was backing out of the wedding today, here and now. She moved aside toward the vestibule. He followed.

"It seems I must apologize now twice." He let amusement come through his voice and was satisfied to see her relax.

"Twice?"

"Yes. First, for alarming you just now. But what I really came to say is that I am sorry for being so abrasive yesterday. I do mean to go on with the marriage. But please forgive my lack of manners."

She smiled. "Let's agree to forgive each other and start over."

He smiled back and held out a hand for her to shake. "It's a deal."

"Miss Foster, there you are," Mrs. Beck trilled as she inserted herself between them. "Come along now. It's time to get ready for the wedding. I'm sure Mr. Stafford will excuse us. The next time you see each other will be at the altar." Mrs. Beck sent a coy glance over her shoulder at Jeremy as she maneuvered Marianne to a side room.

Jeremy bowed and backed up. His eyes caught Marianne's, and he winked. She widened her eyes as she was borne away by Mrs. Beck. Jeremy caught back a laugh.

"Stop mooning. She'll be all yours soon enough." Thad clapped a hand on Jeremy's shoulder. "Come on, Ma and Amelia are sitting toward the front. Come sit with us."

Jeremy caught Robert settling his mother across the room and exchanged nods.

Soon enough, Thad said. Yes, soon enough.

* * *

Marianne let Mrs. Beck bustle her toward the dressing room. She was sure Elinore was right behind her. Meg and the other witnesses were in the hands of another matron.

The jewels flashed, and she remembered that this was Mrs. Hanford. Marianne caught Meg's eye and widened her own in entreaty.

Meg looked to Mrs. Hanford, who was giving directions, and moved closer to Marianne.

Was the room warm? Maybe Marianne would not faint if she had a mind to not do so. Murmurs of conversation swirled around her.

"It will be fine," Meg whispered in her ear as she sidled up next to Marianne.

"Of course it will," Marianne agreed, twisting her reticule in her hands. "He just apologized."

"Apologized?"

"Yes, for his manner yesterday. We agreed to start over."

"I suppose so, since the wedding is going forward."

"Um, yes."

"Come Miss Foster. There is not much time to get you ready for your bridegroom." Mrs. Beck motioned urgently.

Marianne sighed. "See you at the altar, and thank you for your friendship." She hugged Meg quickly and followed Mrs. Beck.

Marianne's mind seemed to be flitting all over the place. She wished she could settle her thoughts somewhere. But maybe that was to be expected at this time. She was soon to marry Jeremy Stafford in front of a crowd of strangers. That, all by itself, was strange.

She wanted her mother. Who was on the other side of the country.

She sighed. Mr. Stafford was still a brown man. She wondered if her wifely duties might extend to wardrobe advisement. Today he wore a brown wool suit. But, she reflected, he had *some* eye to style, since his waistcoat was embroidered in gold. His brown-and-gold tie sat neatly under the collar of his shirt. His mustache had been neatly trimmed. And his hazel eyes were warm.

Her heart skipped a beat. She placed a hand over it.

"Now don't you worry, dear. Everything will be just beautiful. You will see," Mrs. Beck assured her. She pulled Marianne into the dressing room, where Elinore was already in the process of changing. It seemed Mrs. Schulte had taken charge of Elinore.

"Elinore, what a beautiful gown! You look so lovely in it." Marianne took the opportunity to glance over at her fellow bride as Mrs. Beck took away her Sunday dress and shook out her own wedding gown.

"Thank you." Elinore smoothed her hand reverently down her skirt and blushed.

Marianne would have said more, but Mrs. Beck effectively cut off breath and words as she lowered the gown over Marianne's head. There seemed to be no time for conversation as the older ladies readied their brides.

"My dear, you look radiant!" Mrs. Beck exclaimed when she finally stood back to admire her handiwork. "Your gown is exquisite. Did your mother arrange for it? Yes, I see. She must love you very much and wish she could be here. If I may just step in for her for a few moments?"

Marianne startled as Mrs. Beck embraced her gently. The matron slightly swayed in a comforting maternal hug that brought tears to Marianne. She blinked them away as Mrs. Beck stepped back.

She smoothed the soft waves of her dusty rose silk skirt. Her mother might have chosen a husband over her daughter at home, but she'd sent Marianne with a beautiful gown for her wedding. Marianne had insisted that the gown be one she could wear after the wedding. After all, this wasn't a love match that required white lace. But this dress was gorgeous. Her mother knew fashion.

The skirt bustled at the back. She was grateful for the stand-up collar of the matching jacket. The maroon collar and cuffs provided a pleasing contrast of color. An ivory lace jabot fell in soft waves outside the bodice. Pearl beading had been sewn into the bodice and hems of skirt and jacket. A short lace veil sat on her head, where Meg had helped her to pile the curls before church and Mrs. Beck had adjusted a minute ago.

She carried her Bible with a maroon ribbon and a sprig of pine.

December thirteenth. Her wedding day.

"Well, Miss Foster, I won't be calling you that again." Mrs. Beck winked.

And it was time.

Marianne paused after her first step. Oh my. All those eyes staring at her. She jutted out her chin, set her attention forward, and took another step. And another. She felt the tension radiating from Elinore and was thankful they were doing this together.

Helen Dawes played the off-key organ, and the first screech of Minerva Dawes resounded as she began to sing a wedding song. Marianne tried to contain a wince and glanced at Elinore, whose face mirrored her own. They shared a giggle before walking down the aisle together. To that awful noise. Nothing about this day resembled her now faded dreams for her wedding.

As she walked, Marianne's attention was snagged by Jeremy Stafford, her bridegroom, standing straight at the altar, without his stick. His eyes on her.

She caught her breath. She was really going to marry him. A sudden break in the clouds sent a ray of sun through the window, and he stood under its brilliance, his hair shining. Her eyes widened. A sign from God?

The sun disappeared as she came abreast, and she saw a look of awe on his face. For her? Maybe everything would be all right. He gently took her hand, and she let it rest in his. They repeated their vows. Marianne's voice trembled.

"You may now kiss your bride," Preacher Sutton declared, and he turned to Elinore and Robert. Their vows faded into the background as Marianne tensed. Would Jeremy kiss her? The first time in front of all these people?

Jeremy captured her eyes, lifted the hand he had just placed a ring on, turned it over, and kissed her palm. He folded her fingers over it and gently lowered her hand. All the time gazing into her eyes. It felt like a promise. For the hope of an enduring future.

* * *

Jeremy could barely remember anything about the wedding. He could hardly breathe from the moment Marianne started up the aisle toward him. His breath stuck in his throat until he heard her say *I do*. Only then could he let his breath go and draw it again.

Jeremy watched his bride now. The brand-new wedding band that he'd bought from Hanford's Jewelers at the mining office flashed on her hand. His heart galloped as he remembered sharing that intimate look with her as he'd kissed her open palm at the end of the ceremony. The buzz of people all around him barely registered. This lovely creature was now his wife. And she even smiled at him. He returned it, his heart trying to beat out of his chest.

Jeremy wondered if his shoulders would be sore after all the back slapping he had endured today.

"Well, you've gone and done it."

"Did it hurt? Getting shackled?"

"Now the rest of us are truly locked in."

"Congratulations, Man. My turn is coming up."

He leaned against the wall, arms crossed. He propped his stick behind him while he observed the room. The same room that hosted the brides' welcome reception—was that only yesterday? Now it held his and Marianne's, and the Camerons', wedding guests.

He had been shocked by all the people who had come today to watch him and Robert marry their brides. He wondered if most had come out of curiosity. The Busy Bees, as the society leaders were called, had spread the word. Their zeal to grow this town was truly commendable. People rarely said no to them when a project was undertaken. The mail order brides were such a project, and if his own wedding was any indication, the Busy Bees just might get the community populated.

His eyes jerked back to Marianne. Louisa and Amelia McNeil crowded around her, along with several other ladies. Louisa hugged her, and somehow Jeremy felt reassured. Would Marianne be a social butterfly? He already knew she had a determination for her business. And she was a woman who kept her word.

He widened his eyes. Yes, he was sure she had meant to walk away, but here she was.

"You had any food yet?" Thad leaned next to him.

"Nah, not yet. I did get a piece of cake."

"Well, take advantage of the spread over there before you head home. You'll need it." Thad chuckled and Jeremy punched his arm.

"Seriously, man, I think you are already falling for her."

Jeremy didn't respond. He didn't know what he felt.

"Did you notice how full the church was?"

"I confess I was nervous. All I saw was Marianne walking toward me."

"I noticed. I think you will be fine, my friend. I am going to round up the family now so we can get home before it gets much later and colder. I'll be back in a few days. You have my best wishes. Be happy, brother." Thad shook his hand.

The Camerons had left a little while ago. Was it time yet to collect his bride and go home?

* * *

Shouts and cowbells sounded outside the hotel as the new Mr. and Mrs. Stafford began their walk home. Marianne slipped her hand through Jeremy's offered arm. The Busy Bees had arranged for delivery of a basket of food for their private wedding supper at home.

Now Marianne gathered her skirts high to escape mud stains.

"I think it all went well, don't you?" Jeremy tried to walk without a limp as he and Marianne traipsed down the street. He hated that his pole—it seemed to grow—made splashes as they moved along. The streetlamps had been lit, and the wet lane reflected their light. At least the sleet had stopped for now.

Marianne slowed her steps. "Yes, everyone seemed to have a good time. I will miss Meg though. She and her brother left right after the ceremony. I wish she lived here in Wild Rose Ridge. At least Elinore will be close, and we've promised to visit."

"You'll keep in contact with Meg, I am sure." If that was what his lovely wife wanted, Jeremy would do what he could to make sure she maintained communication with her friend. "I'm glad you and Elinore have become friends."

"Yes, I am too."

They walked in silence for a short time, past the bank, the café, then the tailor shop. Marianne shivered, and she seemed to huddle into her muff. Jeremy's mind went blank for conversation, and a prickle of nerves danced down his spine. What would be the expectations of both for the evening—or the night?

"All the shops have Christmas wreaths on their doors," she said. "And the streetlights have pine garlands wound around them. I imagine it is all quite pretty in the daylight."

"It is. The town has several Christmas celebrations. You'll see. And here we are."

Jeremy stopped, his mouth agape.

The outer door to the vestibule shared by both shops hung open. The basket of food had been set to the side. Motioning for Marianne to stand still, he crept inside. A lantern hung by the door for his convenience, and he lit it now and swung it slowly in an arc as he took in the wreckage inside.

Four

Wild Rose Ridge

Jeremy's jaw tightened. He barely kept his bum knees from buckling. Or was it shock? Someone had taken an axe to his work. A chair, with its arms chopped off. Other chairs strewn all over the floor in stages of demolition. A vanity table with drawers pulled out and splintered, and the broken mirror lying to the side of it. Coat racks broken in two and all the arms sliced off. His tools were strewn about. Even a sawhorse showed signs of whacking on it. More lumps lay in corners. He knew what they *had* been.

He felt warmth at his side as Marianne stood next to him.

She put a hand on his arm. "I'm so sorry, Jeremy. Who would do such a terrible thing?"

He knew. Of course he knew. But he would never be able to prove it.

His livelihood. In shambles. And a new bride to support.

He dropped the arm that held the lamp. He needed to

check the other side of the partition to see if the damage extended to Marianne's shop.

"Let's go through here and back to my—our living quarters."

She nodded, backed up, and picked up the food basket. When he moved to take it, she walked ahead of him. He looked at his hands. One held the lamp and the other his stick. He wanted to fling the stick away. But just now he was dependent on it. He hated that. Dependent.

He led the way into her shop and swing the light to see. Nothing here had been disturbed. The glass case that he had special ordered still stood in the middle of the room, dividing front from back. A curtain still hung where he had fixed it into place yesterday. It hid a worktable from future customers. Other things lay in shadows, ready for Marianne to inspect in daylight.

His breath swooshed out. Not all was lost.

Marianne squeezed in behind him, and he moved to accommodate her. She looked around and gasped. He glanced at her face in the gloom. What did she see? Was she displeased?

"Jeremy, this is wonderful." She took a small turn as she looked around. "You captured my vision for a shop. It means much more now, after seeing . . . well—"

"Of course." He said gruffly. "You're welcome. Follow me."

He led her along the partition wall to the back of her shop and through a door to the private space. In the kitchen to the side, a cookstove stood by the back wall. Its warmth spread into the room and into Jeremy's cold limbs. He hung the lantern on the hook by the door, set his stick next to it, and took the basket from Marianne to set it on the table. He moved to the cookstove and bent to retrieve wood from the fire basket and shove it into the stove.

Marianne set her muff next to the basket and surveyed the kitchen. A window gave a ghostly light to the countertop and cupboards below it. A pantry took up a corner space. He watched as she strolled slowly through and into the sitting room.

He gave a mental herculean thrust to his worries over his shop. Right now he needed to care for his new wife. Even as she passed him, he caught a whiff of mock orange blossom. A scent he loved in the late spring. Now it would forever link his wife's presence with him.

Wife. Instant heat diffused in his body. How could he be torn over his shop and what the damage might mean and be so aware of this reaction to his new wife? And at the same time. It was a good thing she couldn't see his face in the darkness. If he felt such intense heat, then his face must be bright red.

"It looks homey," Marianne said as she stood by the stuffed chairs and table that held another lamp and a book.

He hurried to light the lamp, lifting the glass dome to put a match to the wick. Now it looked much more welcoming.

"I hope you will feel at home here. It *is* your home now."

Was that a blush he saw on her face?

"It's a bit bare, I know. But I thought you might have ideas on how you want to change it."

She stood still, just taking it in. Jeremy shifted his feet. He wanted to spend the evening with his brand-new wife. But the shop had to be buttoned up. The door had to be rehung and plywood nailed over the hole where it had been kicked in. The window had been broken, and he needed to seal it up before he turned in.

But he had to make sure Marianne was safe and comfortable first.

"The, uh, sleeping quarters are through the door here."

* * *

Marianne wondered if he could see her blush. She could feel it deepening as he showed her into another room. He seemed to be in a hurry to usher her this direction. Would she have to have that "talk" with him now? The one where she insisted that they get to know each other first?

"Your trunk is through here." He picked up the lantern and again led the way slowly. Now her whole body blushed. She wanted to wipe her face but kept her hands at her sides.

Jeremy had hung a couple of curtains to divide the room. He pushed aside one of the curtains to show her a bed, a washstand with a pitcher, bowl and a stack of towels, a small dresser with a mirror, and a wardrobe and her trunk.

"I thought you might like some privacy," he muttered as he set the lantern on the dresser and brushed by her without looking back as he left the room. She nearly sagged from relief.

"Jeremy." Her voice arrested him. "Thank you. You are very thoughtful."

"I want you to be comfortable." He ducked his head and let the curtain fall, and she heard noises from the other side.

He must be changing his clothes. Would she never stop blushing? She wanted to get changed herself. The wedding clothes had served their purpose, and now real life must set in.

Marianne stood in the middle of her portion of the sleeping quarters until Jeremy left the room and she heard him moving about in the kitchen. She couldn't bring herself to think of this room as a bedroom. She wasn't ready for that kind of intimacy. She suspected Jeremy wasn't either. His movements had been rather jerky. It had nothing to do with his physical disability. If she didn't feel so strange herself, she might find that amusing.

She had better get to the business of changing her clothes now. Turning to her trunk, which had been delivered earlier, she searched for a more comfortable skirt and shirtwaist. She took off her lace jabot and laid it on the quilt covering the bed. She paused to smooth her fingers over the colorful wedding ring quilt. Its beauty made her wonder about the creator of this fine work. She would not have expected a man alone to have such a quilt.

She heard the grates clash as Jeremy probably stuffed more wood into the cookstove box for heat. She shivered. The kitchen and sitting room had been warm enough, but the chill in here sent goose bumps up her arms now.

She hurried to take off the silk jacket and skirt. She untied the bustle next and dropped it onto the bed. And paused.

Oh no.

Why had she not thought of this before? How was she going to unlace the corset and get it off? Why hadn't she put on the front lace corset this morning? Well, because that wouldn't have worked at all with her fancy gown.

Reaching behind her, she felt for the laces. She could barely find them. And she could *not* find the ends to pull to unlace them. How many grommets were there to unlace?

Oh no, no, no.

She certainly was not cold any longer. She would have

to ask for help. From a man. That she didn't know. Even if he was her husband.

Marianne looked for her dressing gown. Could that cover her well enough for him to unlace her yet preserve her modesty? Somehow? She pulled it on backward over her arms and shoulders and held it at the base of her back. At least her chemise gave her a modicum of protection. Well, maybe she could manage this way.

What was he going to think? What had he last said? He wanted her to be comfortable.

She paced as she held the dressing gown together. She swallowed. Paced some more. He probably wondered what was keeping her. She had to call him in.

"Jeremy?"

"Yes? Are you all right?"

"I am. But I'm afraid I need some help."

And then he was there. Anxiety radiated from him, and she watched as his shoulders bunched even tighter as he took in her state of undress.

She turned her back to him.

"Please." She couldn't get anything else out of her dried-up throat.

He cleared his own throat, and she felt his fumbling at her back. Now she shivered for a different reason.

"I'm sorry it got so cold in here. I promise it will warm up soon," he said hoarsely.

"I know." His fingers were now halfway up her back. She couldn't breathe.

Then the corset slipped and Jeremy hurried out of the room. Marianne fell onto the bed, the annoying garment lying over her chemise, with her dressing gown. She covered her face with her hands and took deep breaths before thrusting the offending corset aside.

Sitting up, Marianne blessed herself for her foresight. Mama would have sent a lot of useless dresses that required corsets like this. But Marianne now considered herself a businesswoman and had invested in a variety of shirtwaists and serviceable skirts. She would avoid back-laced corsets like the plague. Thank goodness she had the ordinary ones that she could manage for herself.

Dressed now in a green-and-white-striped shirtwaist and a dark- green skirt, Marianne thrust the fancy corset in a corner of her trunk and shook her head at the lacy night-gown that Mama had slipped in for a wedding night. If only Mama could know. Ah no, Mama should not know how this day had turned out.

Marianne hung the lavish gown and jacket in the wardrobe and grabbed a shawl. Turning, she looked more closely at the small dresser took on a cozy glow in the light of the lantern. She noted the carved posts on the bed. She had not paid attention to the wardrobe before, but now she saw its intricate shaping. Had Jeremy made everything? A rush of warmth went through her that had nothing to do with a blush.

This kind man had prepared for his bride.

* * *

Jeremy willed his thoughts away from the woman in the other room. A little while ago he couldn't think of anything but the damage to the shop. Now he couldn't get that enticing picture of his bride out of his mind. He almost hadn't been able to grasp those laces in his trembling hands. And she *was* his wife. So could his thoughts be wrong?

Yes, he decided, they could. For now.

He busied himself by emptying the food basket. The

Busy Bees had made sure to send plenty from the wedding feast. He and Marianne would have a good couple of meals.

Marianne came into the kitchen calmly. He peered at her under his brows. Her face was red, but that was the only sign of her embarrassment. Okay, he could pretend too.

If only he could get that picture of her out of his mind from the bedroom. And stop the heat from rolling up his neck. He noted her serviceable attire.

"Are you hungry?" she asked, taking in the array of dishes on the table.

"Not especially. I want to get into the shops to shut them up against the weather. But I thought I should unpack the basket if you would like to eat."

She moved to put the colder foods into the icebox. Then turned to him.

"I am going to help you."

"No need. This is your first night here. Please feel free to relax or go to bed." His bride should not have to be working on her wedding night.

"Jeremy, we may not know each other very well yet, but I do know you are going to go into your shop to secure it before retiring for the night." Marianne crossed her arms. "We are married now. I plan to stand by your side in bad times as well as good times. Now, let's go out there and do what needs to be done for tonight."

Jeremy stared at her. She stared back.

"All right, then." He turned to the door, and she followed him. Grabbing the lantern he marched out.

"You don't need your stick?"

"No."

A sudden tension developed, and Jeremy knew he'd been too abrupt. This marriage thing was going to take some getting used to. He softened his tone. "I don't use it so much at home or in the shop. I know where things are."

"But things are strewn all over now, and it's dark."

"It's all right, Marianne," he said gruffly, and she offered no other comment. He held the light high so both could see. It wouldn't do to trip over anything after being so definite.

They turned the corner from her shop and into his. Jeremy stopped, and his heart stuttered again. So much damage. How could he possibly recover? Some Christmas commissions would be undeliverable.

But he could not dwell on that. He was aware of Marianne's presence behind him. His pride would not allow him to show weakness in front of her. He already had a strike—no, make that two strikes—against him with his knees. He had to show her strength now. Especially now.

The outer door hung crooked. The inner door to his shop needed the hole in it to be covered. His window had to be covered as well. Thank God the porch overhang kept most of the freezing rain out. But the wind whistled in and brought some dampness with it.

Marianne silently stepped forward and held out her hand for the lantern. Jeremy passed it to her and strode closer to the outer door. He examined the hinges, then turned to see if he could scrounge any new ones in his supplies.

As he moved, Marianne tried to anticipate where to hold the lantern. He appreciated her efforts. Now standing still, Jeremy inspected what he could see in the dim light. It appeared that his cupboards were undisturbed, and his drawers looked normal.

"Over here," he instructed, and they moved to the

cupboards. He yanked out a drawer and let out a sigh. Yes, he had extra hinges.

Walking slowly to avoid any unseen objects in his way, Jeremy returned to the door with tools and hinges, Marianne following.

He hesitated. He hated to ask her. A lady shouldn't have to do this kind of manual labor.

"Do you need some help holding the door while you change those hinges?" she asked, already hanging the lantern on the hook by the door.

Resignation spread across his face. "I suppose you already figured you had an answer for that question."

She tipped her head to the side with a sassy look on her face. "It is rather obvious."

With a half grin, he strode to the door and pushed it against the frame. "If you can just hold it here, I'll get the old hinges off. Let me know if it is too heavy."

"Uh- huh. What will you do if it is?" She placed her hands against the door, keeping it in place.

"How good are you with screws and drivers?"

"Never used them."

"Then you are stuck with holding the door."

"I'll manage it."

Once the outer door was again in place, Jeremy nailed boards against the hole in the door leading to his area.

Marianne shivered.

"Are you all right?" he asked her as he straightened up and dropped his hammer to his side. "You can go back to the warmth of the living quarters now if you like."

"No, I will stay here and help you as long as you need it." She grabbed the lantern from the hook and gripped it closer to the window for Jeremy to work.

"Stubborn woman," he muttered as he fixed a board

across the broken glass. He caught a faint smile on her face and stopped to return it. He was grateful for her help.

"Well, that should do it for now." He pounded in the last nail, and the wind was whistling outside now.

Or maybe that was something else outside?

A loud mocking laugh sounded through the cracks.

"Don't think this is over, Stafford." A shout accompanied the laughter. "That bride should have been Aichen's, not yours!"

Five

Loud pounding startled Marianne awake the next morning. Faint light came through her small window, and she looked around at the unfamiliar surroundings. More pounding, and her heart answered with its own pounding.

"What the—" She heard Jeremy grunt and his feet hit the ground.

"Jeremy?"

"Stay here."

Marianne wanted to jump up and run after him as he left the room. She quelled the alarm that raced through her. Maybe she would feel safer with him than alone. Was he going to be ordering her around? She'd see about that.

On the other hand, she was new in town. Staying put might be the best thing to do for now. Especially after the shout and laughter she'd heard last night from that unknown man. He'd sounded drunk, and Jeremy had confirmed that the man spent a lot of time in the saloon. Jeremy had that she should not concern herself with that man.

The pounding ceased. Since the hammering came from the other side of the wall from where she lay, she surmised that Jeremy must have entered his shop and discovered the source.

Wondering what was happening just now with half her brain, the other half insisted on concerning itself with the man from last night. Did that incident have anything to do with this morning's disturbance? She surely didn't appreciate the comment about whose bride she should be. She could figure that out for herself.

Who was Aichen anyway?

Deciding that lying here was doing no good, Marianne shoved her covers aside and put her feet on the floor. She shivered. She was glad she had packed cotton night dresses, and that the lace thing was still in the trunk.

The noise resumed.

Marianne scrambled into the same clothes she'd worn last night and hurried into the kitchen to feed the stove fire.

She hesitated. She needed to visit the necessary, but was it safe? How would she find out? Jeremy had escorted her last night before they'd retired, so she knew it was out the back door. What would be best? What if Jeremy needed help?

Her needs could wait. She entered the hall leading to her shop. No activity. She wanted to linger and examine what Jeremy had built for her, but the thumping and battering noises grew louder, and she hurried to the front, where the entry split between the two shops.

She came to a halt, and her eyes took in mass chaos. Or so it seemed.

Jeremy, his hair still sticking out from sleep, stood in the center of the room, pointing and shouting. He was directing the chaos, Marianne realized. The window had been uncovered, and the chill reached her. She rubbed both arms.

Men were everywhere. Some breaking apart what looked like furniture pieces and others repairing them. Some order was coming from a chopped-up mess. Stacks of what appeared to be firewood lay against the wall. Some had intricate carving on them. Marianne closed her eyes for a moment. What Jeremy must be feeling to have his hard work hacked up like this.

Her eyes found him again. His eyes snagged on hers, and they stared at each other a moment. A tingle of awareness skittered down her spine. He jutted his chin at her and turned to respond to one of the men.

How could she ever have thought him short and small? In spite of his unruly hair, he appeared very much in command of the situation. He still limped as he thrust objects out of his way, but his determination to clear the mess drove his actions.

She could feel safe with a man like this. He didn't allow setbacks to defeat him.

Thank you, God, for directing my path this way.

Thad McNeil spotted her and raised a hand in greeting. She nodded back to him and backed away from the scene. Nature was making itself known.

"Oh good, you are up and about." Mrs. McNeil and her daughter Amelia stood in the doorway, scanning the room, then eyeing Marianne. "I hope you were able to rest last night in spite of this." Her arm swept toward the men working.

"Oh yes. We did finally get some rest." Marianne blushed. She wished she could recall her words and say something else. It sounded like she and Jeremy had spent the night together. Well, they did, but not like *that*. Her blush deepened, and Mrs. McNeil's eyes sparkled.

Mrs. McNeil held a basket in front of her. "We brought food. Other ladies are coming with food as well. Perhaps we could enter your shop instead of this one?"

"Oh, of course." As Marianne backed into her own empty shop, Mrs. McNeil followed her and looked around. Marianne left ajar the door from her shop to the street so ladies would not need to step around the carpentry shop mess. Amelia lingered, her gaze still on the brawny figures hard at work.

"Come along, dear. We will need your help."

"Yes, Mama. Coming." Amelia winked, and Marianne smiled in amusement. It would appear that Amelia was not a shy young miss after all.

Mrs. McNeil put the basket on the glass counter that would soon house Marianne's wares. "There. This is suitable for spreading food upon. Do you have some rags for us to wipe it?"

"I'll find some." Marianne's bladder was near to bursting. She hurried to the back of the building. She erupted out the back door and ran to the privy. *Just in time.* What would Mrs. McNeil think of her?

"Oh my lands." She sighed as she walked into the kitchen to find cleaning items. After this, she would find the privy *first* before she could embarrass herself further.

"How did you know what happened?" Marianne asked as she came back to Mrs. McNeil and Amelia. The curtain separating the space had been rolled back to the wall, exposing the worktable. Two surfaces were available for spreading food on today.

"Miss O'Malley arranged for a basket of food to be

delivered to your door last night. That way you and Jeremy could have a romantic stroll home from the hotel. The next thing we knew, the porter ran back into the hotel to tell us that Jeremy's shop was broken into and things inside were smashed as far as he could see."

"But how would that bring people today?"

Mrs. McNeil paused and studied Marianne. Amelia gaped. Marianne felt somehow exposed but not sure what she had said.

"My dear girl, we are a community here that cares for one another. At first glance we look like a small Western town with not much to recommend us but a beautiful lake. But the people here support one another. Is that not so where you come from?"

Marianne rubbed her cloth across the top of the worktable. "I'm afraid not. I come from a city where people get lost." Who had come around to help her and Mama when Papa had died and left them with few funds? Enough to find a modest home if they could sell the mansion. But mostly, society suddenly disappeared. Until Mr. Wonderful came along and married Mama and banished Marianne.

"You poor dear." Mrs. McNeil came around the counter and hugged Marianne, then put her hands on her shoulders. "You are one of us now. Welcome."

Marianne searched the face of this motherly woman. "Thank you."

"Well now, let's get started setting out the food. The other ladies will be here soon. Oh, before I forget, we need to chat about upholstering some chairs for your parlor when Jeremy gets them built." The older lady bustled about finishing the counter wiping, inside as well as on top.

"Oh, ah, yes."

"She does tend to take charge. But she is very mild in

her bossiness compared to the Busy Bees," Amelia whispered in Marianne's ear. "Just to warn you."

"The Busy Bees . . ."

"Yes, otherwise known as community leaders. It was they who concocted the idea to send for mail order brides. They think the bachelors here need settling down." Amelia laughed softly.

"Do they?"

Amelia cocked her head to one side. "Well, maybe."

* * *

Marianne wanted to cover her ears with her hands. The Dawes ladies thought they knew just how Marianne should set up her shop. Every time they opened their mouths, Marianne could still hear the screeching voice and instrument from yesterday's services.

Mrs. Beck had come right behind them. After setting her food basket on the counter, she had not been shy about airing her opinions either.

"Over here a table would look lovely. When the carpentry shop is put to rights, Mr. Stafford could make one," A Dawes sister said.

"Oh, no, Minerva. This is not a home parlor. She will need something shimmery here to set off hats. You are making hats, are you not, my dear?" Mrs. Beck glanced at Marianne. An answer was not expected. "A rack to set off shawls. Yes, of course. Can't you just see them draping here?" Mrs. Beck moved to a corner by the window.

"Adelaide, Mrs. Stafford will be making and featuring hats. You said so yourself. A rack for shawls should not be in a prime spot."

"Now, Helen, there's no need to be snippy. Shawls do go with hats, after all." Mrs. Beck huffed.

Marianne's head swiveled from one to the other as they bustled about, not really accomplishing anything. Their packed food baskets still sat unopened. She looked to the carpentry shop and back to the baskets. She caught Mrs. McNeil shaking her head and rolling her eyes as she unpacked the baskets. Amelia raised an eyebrow at Marianne, who was glad for the earlier heads up. They both stifled giggles.

Val O'Malley walked in with a couple of boxes of desserts. She looked around until she found Marianne and grinned. She set the boxes on the counter and moved around it.

"I see some of the Bees are here and already getting you set up."

"You heard them?"

"Yes, coming in. Maybe they'll have some good ideas for you." She laughed. "How are things going next door?" Without waiting for an answer, Val walked to the dividing hallway and peered in.

"Come, ladies. We need to fill these makeshift tables with food. The men will be in here soon, hungry as bears. I'm sure Marianne will furnish her shop as she sees fit in due time." Mrs. McNeil's dry comment brooked no argument. The other ladies gathered around the counter and set out the feast.

Marianne had never seen so many tubs of mashed potatoes and bowls of gravy. Roast beef, fried chicken, and several kinds of canned fruits and vegetables and bread rounded out the meal. She had been tasked with stacking plates and cutlery at the beginning of the layout.

"This is so generous," Marianne stood back to look at the steaming food.

"Your husband is well regarded, Mrs. Stafford." Mrs. Beck came to stand next to Marianne. "When disasters happen, we come together to fix it. You'll see."

"So I've been told," Marianne murmured and stood back against a wall as Mrs. McNeil ushered the men in to eat. Marianne expected them to push and shove their way in, but even as they jested and mock insulted each other, they politely filed in.

"Gather around, gents. Let us pray." Preacher Sutton folded his hands at his waist. "Lord God, we thank thee for this bounty and for those who have assembled it for us. We ask thee to bless this house and bring comfort and order to the chaos visited upon it. We pray for peace. Amen."

Men crowded one another as they grabbed for plates to fill.

Marianne watched as Jeremy filled his plate. He looked around, and when his gaze stopped on her, he slowly made his way next to her. He leaned against the wall, his plate in front of him.

"Not quite the way you expected to meet the town, is it?" He smiled at her and scooped up potatoes.

"Not exactly. But I've been hearing how everyone helps one another in this town. And I see it displayed right here. Thank you for bringing me." Marianne had not realized how deep her gratitude had settled into her soul until just now. She felt his penetrating gaze. But he continued to eat. Why did she feel relieved?

"How is everything going?" she asked.

He swallowed. "Yeah, well we're getting it cleaned up."

"What about the window?"

His lips firmed. "One of the fellas measured it and ran

across the street to the mercantile to make a rush order to get a new window in. Should only be a few days—it can be on the *Merry Jo* with the next delivery."

"So it will stay boarded up until then." She made it a statement, not a question, and he nodded.

"I see the preacher is here too." Marianne noticed that Val had grabbed a plate of food and chatted with Preacher Sutton. What could be going on there?

"Hmm. Are you going to eat?"

"Yes, of course. Does the sheriff have any idea who did this?"

Jeremy shifted. Did his knees bother him? There was nowhere to sit yet. Or maybe he was reluctant to discuss what happened to his shop. But she was his wife, after all, and she should know.

"I don't think so."

Marianne stared at him. Jeremy scraped his plate clean and stood away from the wall.

"We'll talk later. Right now we must finish up for today before it gets dark. Thank you for the food. Please tell the ladies for me, would you?"

And he left her looking after him.

Yes indeed, they would talk later.

* * *

Jeremy looked over the table in their living quarters. He ran a hand over his face and dropped into a chair and stared. So much food. His gratitude knew no bounds. *Thank you, Lord, for the wonderful people in this town.*

The day had been full. Lots of people doing so much to help him and his bride over a rough patch. What a way to start a marriage. *In good times and in bad.*

He looked up as Marianne sat across from him. She, too, looked worn out. Her once crisp blouse and skirt hung limply on her. He couldn't help but notice that her beauty was not in the least diminished, even as a few strands of her glorious dark hair escaped the knot on her head to flow freely about her face.

You are still here, Lord. You have blessed me so mightily. My shop may be in shambles, but You have brought me such a beautiful companion.

"What are you thinking?"

He started. Oops. He must have been staring at her.

"Oh nothing. Just that this day turned out nothing like I expected."

She smiled. "I completely agree."

He held out a hand, palm up. She looked at it, then up to his face.

"Let's pray for our meal. It is our first one alone as a married couple."

She flushed and put her hand in his. Perhaps her family didn't pray before meals? He meant to start well. He prayed for the meal, and they passed dishes back and forth.

"Since I had so much help today, let's you and I do tomorrow what I planned for today."

"And what is that?"

"A walk around town. I don't believe you have seen it in the daylight yet. I'd like for you to know where everything is. The mercantile is across the street and up one. I'm sure you will have plenty of use for that store." He grinned and took a long gulp of water. When did he get so thirsty? "Feel free to order whatever you need. I'm sure Phineas Prentiss, the storekeeper, will be happy to help you."

They ate silently for a few minutes. Then Jeremy scraped back his chair and leaned against the back of it.

"What did you mean when you thanked me for bringing you here at lunch today?"

Her startled gaze flew to his. "What are you talking about?"

"You said something about learning how our town helps one another and thanked me for bringing you here. What did you mean?"

She lowered her head, rose, and picked up dishes to take to the washstand. She paused, came back for more, then stood by the table. He waited.

She looked up and around the room with a sigh before her shadowed eyes met his. His heart stuttered somewhere inside his chest. His Marianne had been wounded.

His Marianne.

"When my father died, he left us with little. We could sell the mansion, but we would lose all the friends we had. Such is society. Mama tried to marry me off to some of the older men with deep pockets." Her words were matter of fact, as if they had happened to someone else.

She sat down and rested one arm on the table and the other in her lap.

Still, he waited.

"I told her she should marry them herself." She lifted her head. "Not a nice thing to say to one's mother."

He covered her hand with his own. "It's all right, Marianne. It sounds like a difficult time for you and your mother."

She took a deep breath. "Yes. Well, she did."

"Did what?"

Marianne made a face at him. "She married one of them."

"Oh."

"I can't blame her. She has to look out for her elder

years. Who would take care of her? At least, that's how she saw it. Her new husband made it very clear to both of us that he married *her* and had no intentions of supporting anyone else. I had to go." Marianne's hand fluttered slightly under his.

"Mama made sure I had a nice trousseau. I made sure I had a working wardrobe, and we looked at several marriage brokers. The one in Chicago, The Sisters Mail Order Bride Company, sounded the best. They had an informational tea and an escort service—that is Miss O'Malley—to bring us as a group to our destination. Now you know."

He was silent, not sure what to say. He rubbed a thumb across her hand, trying to offer her support.

"Do you think God orchestrates our lives?"

His hold on her hand tightened and suddenly his throat constricted. "Yes, I do."

She nodded. "All right, then. This was my story. Now I have a new one. With you. Do you know why your shop was destroyed? Or who shouted at us last night?"

He let go of her hand and sat back again. She didn't beat about the bush. He wondered how to respond to such a direct demand. He intended to protect her and not cause more worry. But her determined look said she would not let it go. He studied her face.

Before he could think, he heard himself say, "Last night was just the rumblings of a drunken logger. Or at least, he used to be a logger. Nothing more than that. Don't worry about him."

"I didn't like what he said about me being somebody else's bride, like I'm chattel to be passed around."

"Of course not. No one would like that. But as I said, he's a drunk and spends a lot of time at the saloon."

"And your shop?"

He swallowed. "I don't know. The sheriff has a report. I'm sure he will find out for us."

She scrutinized him, and he kept his return look steady. He would deal with Kircher in his own way, and he would not have his beautiful bride hurt again. Not if he could help it.

Six

Marianne straightened the slight bustle under her brown walking skirt as she slipped on her coat. She had paired this skirt with an ivory shirtwaist with small colorful flowers spritzed on it. Last, she set a matching brown hat on her head. She stifled a giggle. Today she was a brown girl. To match her brown husband. Meg would laugh.

"I'm ready," she announced and picked up her reticule and an umbrella. She surreptitiously looked Jeremy over. Yes, he wore his brown clothes today. She would make sure to expand his wardrobe. At least when they went out together.

"Well then, let's go." He grabbed his stick and opened the door for her to slip through before him.

They walked the stretch of her empty shop and paused in the small vestibule between their shops. Jeremy glanced through his portion of the building. Marianne's gaze followed. Piles of jagged wood lay stacked along the inside wall. Other pieces of furniture that looked salvage-able stood around. His tools were once more hung neatly on the outer walls or arranged on tables above drawers. At least the drawers had not been touched by the destroyer.

"It looks so much better than yesterday," she offered softly.

He grunted and turned to the street door they shared, moving back for her to precede him.

Marianne shivered as she stepped outdoors and snuggled her hands deeper into her muff. The overcast sky parted slightly to allow a pale sun to peek through as clouds floated by. The cold seemed to have frozen some of the mud in the street. She was grateful for that.

Jeremy locked the door behind him and offered his arm while stabbing his stick in the ground with the other. He paused them, looking both directions.

"Let's start at the mercantile," he suggested, and tramped off the boardwalk.

Their own building was at the edge of town. A whiff from the butcher shop and stock holding pens by the river slithered by her nose. She wrinkled it.

"This is my first real look at the town, Jeremy. In the daylight, I mean." Marianne observed the area. Mostly clapboard or log buildings protruded from the ground. Up the street, on the same side as her shop, she saw a rose and white-striped awning. The hotel stood at the end. She had seen glimpses of the lake from the hotel windows.

He considered; his mouth pursed in thought. "I know. I hope it makes a favorable impression on you. I had hoped to take you on this small tour yesterday."

Jeremy steered her past the barbershop and bathhouse that sat directly across from their own shops. Not many comings and goings there on a Tuesday midday. Marianne's eyes slid past them to their destination.

"I think, perhaps, it will. I look forward to seeing the lake."

"And you shall. Here we are at the mercantile." Jeremy waited for her to step up to the boardwalk before carefully lifting his knees to join her. "I promise to bring you back another day to actually shop, but today I just want to acquaint you with the town." He glanced up. "It looks like the weather just might cooperate with us."

"As to the weather, it is still cold." Marianne lifted her hands in her muff. "But at least it is not raining or snowing. A good day for walking."

Really. Their conversation was reduced to the weather?

"Mr. and Mrs. Stafford, how nice to see you." They turned around to see a substantial lady sparkling with jewelry. Marianne's eyes were caught by the feathers and broaches in her hat, more broaches at the collar of her coat, and showy rings on the gloves that covered her fingers.

"I see you are getting along nicely, Mr. Stafford."

Jeremy opened his mouth, but the lady rushed on as she turned to Marianne. Jeremy moved off to converse with the storekeeper.

"I was hoping for a moment to meet you, dear. I'm sure you are confused with so many new faces this week. I am the doctor's wife, Ima Paine."

Marianne widened her eyes, and she quelled a bubble of laughter.

The lady's eyes responded to her humor. "Yes, you may laugh. My name is certainly a town joke, though my husband's profession is not. Welcome to Wild Rose Ridge." She held out a hand to shake.

Marianne placed hers into it for a brief touch. "Please forgive me. You took me rather by surprise. My stay here has been eventful so far."

"I have heard. Please accept both my congratulations on your marriage and my condolences concerning Mr. Stafford's business."

"Thank you."

"Do you have any idea yet when your own shop will be open? You can't imagine how much the ladies in town are looking forward to having a millinery shop. New hats and gloves and so much more. The mercantile is necessary, but Mr. Prentiss really has no idea what ladies want or need." This was said in a conspiratorial whisper as Mrs. Paine looked toward the front of the store, where Jeremy stood talking with the shopkeeper.

Marianne smiled. "My shop will be open as soon as I can set it up, Mrs. Paine. I hope you will be satisfied with what you will find there."

"Oh, I am sure that I will, my dear. And now I must rush away. My husband is waiting for a few things, and I had better get them to him pronto. Our sheriff is sick with a reaction to a cookie. My goodness. How quickly it happened. He's on the mend now, though, but I must go. You have a lovely day with that nice husband of yours."

"I will." Marianne blushed. Did everyone imagine what her marriage might be like? "It was nice to meet you," she called to the lady, who sped to the cash register by the front door of the mercantile.

Jeremy shook hands with Mr. Prentiss and met Marianne on the boardwalk as the doctor's wife departed the mercantile. Marianne adjusted her cold fingers in the muff, searching for the warm spot from just a moment ago. It certainly was December, after all.

Jeremy paused to look back at the store entrance. "Mrs. Paine can be overwhelming sometimes, but she and Doc

Paine pulled me through when my knees were crushed. It was a long recovery. I'll always be grateful to them."

Marianne's hand shot out from her muff again, and she squeezed his arm, though he might not feel it through his coat. "She seemed a caring soul. A bit glittery, but then some color on a cold, gray day is refreshing."

Jeremy grinned as he met her smile.

People crisscrossed the street as they conducted their business between shops. Marianne hoped she would become an accepted citizen of this town. Men dipped hats and women waved at them, and Jeremy dipped his chin or nodded back.

"Oh! Clara! I'm so sorry I nearly bumped into you." Marianne came to an abrupt halt as she greeted the young brown-haired woman, who was leaning on the end of an umbrella, its point resting on the boardwalk, and contemplating the building in front of her. A fellow mail order bride she'd traveled with from Chicago.

Clara turned to greet Marianne and slid her eyes to Jeremy and back. Marianne hastened to introduce them, and Jeremy moved a discreet distance away.

"So how are you faring?" Clara's sincere concern warmed Marianne's heart.

"Well. He is so very kind. I find I have married a man who can rise above obstacles. That is so comforting. Thank you for the small cakes you baked for us for the wedding reception. They are delicious, and we are still eating them. If you are planning on opening a bakery, I think you will have great success."

Clara nodded and peeked at the building beside them.

"I'm so sorry to hear about your intended being sick. Who would have thought Sheriff Goodwin would react so much to your wonderful strawberry cookies? We started out with high hopes from Chicago."

Clara shifted a bundle in her arms. "Does the whole town know?"

Marianne put an arm around her. "This is a small town. Word is bound to get around. But I met Mrs. Paine a little while ago and heard it from her."

Clara sighed. "Sheriff Goodwin and I are trying to figure things out. If he recovers, I suppose Val and the agency's goal is to marry those of us not yet wedded at the Christmas Eve dance. Will you be attending?"

Marianne smiled at Jeremy, and he returned it. She could almost feel the sparkles between them in the shared smile. She needed to rejoin him. She would examine that eagerness later.

She turned back to Clara, her smile still in place. "Of course we will. I like Sheriff Goodwin. He seems to be a good man and a friend to Jeremy. I'm sure he will be fine. I hear that Doc Paine is a good doctor. I must go now, but I'll keep you in my prayers."

"Thank you." Clara closed the distance between herself and the window to squint to see inside.

Marianne watched her for a moment. This could be Clara's dream, then? She would love having one of her bride friends close by.

She linked her arm in Jeremy's again. How comfortable that felt.

"She came on the *Merry Jo* with you?"

"Yes. Sheriff Goodwin is her intended. Mrs. Paine told me when we saw her outside of the mercantile a while ago that he'd reacted to cookies Clara made. I'm sure she's feeling awful."

"The sheriff is a good man. We need him around here. I hope his recovery is quick."

"From what I heard, he is already better. Clara is the one who made the cakes for us."

Jeremy swiveled to glance back a moment at Clara. "Well then, my estimation of her has risen astronomically. How can we get more treats like that?"

She laughed. "Unless I miss my guess, she will be baking for everyone right up the street from us one of these days."

"I approve."

From there they passed the Hanford Mining Office, a cheery Christmas wreath on the door, before Jeremy steered her between The Ridge Hotel and the Courthouse buildings toward the lake. She looked back at the silhouette of the porch wrapping around the hotel and wondered how many of the brides were still there besides Clara.

Mindful of softer ground and Jeremy's gait, Marianne walked slowly.

Suddenly Wild Rose Lake spread out before her, and she stood transfixed at the vista. Waves rolled lightly under the drifting clouds above. As if painted in shades of gray, the landscape showcased the mystery of God. Now and then, clouds would break slightly to allow a pale sun to send a beam into the water before it disappeared just as abruptly. Snowcapped hills rose steeply, the valleys between them darker shadows. In the distance, the blurry form of an island seemed to jut out of the water in the middle of the lake.

Jeremy moved close behind and spoke softly into her ear. His mustache tickled and she shivered, but this had nothing to do with the cold.

"I come here to think. This is where I feel most close to God."

"I can understand that," she answered quietly. Peace permeated the place. Jeremy's nearness warmed her down to her toes, and she didn't move. She didn't even breathe.

* * *

Jeremy inhaled the mock orange scent of Marianne's hair. *I can't help falling in love with you.* He should be dazed or shocked by this realization. He'd only spent two days with her, but he knew her.

"To your left tis a ridge where roses bloom wild in the spring. Wild roses are everywhere around here, but this ridge blooms pink. If you haven't yet heard, it's how the town got its name. I'll take you there come spring."

"I would love that." Her words were low, and he leaned closer to hear her. And smiled. He had to bend his head awkwardly under the brim of her hat, but it was no sacrifice.

They stood like that for a few minutes, and a gust of wind nearly tossed them off their feet. Marianne grabbed for her hat, and her hand came into contact with Jeremy's head. He, in turn, made a grab for his hat. He caught it, and Marianne's hatpins held fast. They laughed, and Jeremy took the opportunity to put an arm around his bride to steady her. Oh, how he would like to do that anytime.

Patience, man.

"I think we should walk on to Betty's Café now. I'm hungry—how about you?" He asked.

"We just had a nudge in that direction. Maybe that's a good idea." She turned, and their eyes caught for a moment.

He glanced at her lips and away at the lake. Not now. It was too early. And she surely would not want to be kissed for the first time where others could see them. He swallowed and turned her to walk in front of him.

Back between buildings. Across the street. By the bank.

"The bank is owned by the Becks, isn't it?" Marianne's question jarred him back to the present—in a practical way. He preferred to dream about his wife.

"Uh, yes. The same Mrs. Beck who has been so helpful to us."

She sent an amused grin his way. "And she has been too. And very kind to me."

"For which I will always be grateful to her," he responded gallantly. "And here we are."

The red-ribboned pine bough wreath on the door clashed with the rose-and-white-striped awning above them as they entered the café. But no one cared. At Christmas, red and green went with everything. Jeremy caught his stick under his arm and opened the door for Marianne to pass through.

Jeremy paused to scout out a table. Yes, there was one by the fireplace. The log beams around it held the warmth and the table was cozy. He helped Marianne shed her coat and draped it over the extra chair and then slid his own on top of it. She set her muff on its seat as he sat down opposite her.

"Well now, if it isn't one of the newest wedded couples in town. I'd hoped you'd drop by." A short, plump woman in a black dress and apron appeared at their table. Her silver-streaked dark hair was caught in a top knot on her head. Her eyes rested first on Jeremy with affection, then inquiringly on Marianne.

"Marianne, this is Betty. She owns the café and takes care of all of us poor bachelors. Betty—"

Betty's eyebrows lifted. "Bachelor, is it?"

Jeremy flushed and met amusement in Marianne's eyes. "Uh, the *other* bachelors. I mean." He sat back, laughing. "You both know what I mean."

Marianne held out her hand, and Betty shook it.

"Nice to meet ya, Mrs. Stafford. He means, I tell all these crusty boys when they need to clean up. And I insist on it. Before they sit down and eat my food."

"Aw, Betty, we all know you love us."

Betty sniffed.

"What's on the menu today?"

"Pork chops and potatoes."

Jeremy grinned at Marianne. "What sounds good to you today?"

"Pork chops and potatoes sound wonderful." she grinned back at him and up at Betty.

"Well, Betty, I think we will have pork chops and potatoes," Jeremy said, and Betty met his eyes with a twinkle in her own.

"Coming right up. Now you two behave while I'm dishing up." Betty hurried away.

Jeremy relaxed. His knees were aching after all the walking that afternoon. He might be in for a sleepless night. He looked at Marianne's concerned face. He must be terrible at hiding his emotions.

"I'm fine. I don't want you worrying about anything."

She nodded, and the line in her forehead smoothed out. She must be better at controlling feelings than he was.

"There aren't many people in here right now. Do they come later?"

"Yes—in another hour the place will be packed. Men getting off work will be looking for their dinner."

"Of course. And we want to be done and away before then?"

"Yes."

"Here you are. Today's special. Enjoy. Good to see you in here again, Jeremy. And good to meet you, Mrs. Stafford."

"Marianne."

"Marianne." Betty bustled away.

Finishing her meal, Marianne glanced around. She couldn't shake a feeling of being watched. Her eyes landed on a scruffy man with a full beard glaring at them from a shadowy corner table.

Jeremy looked up, suddenly alert, and followed her look. Tension tightened his face. As Jeremy returned the stare, the man rose, slapped money on his table, and snarled as he passed their table and left the café.

"Jeremy?"

He forced a tight smile out of a tight jaw. She stiffened.

"You about ready to go? If we plan to get anything done tonight, we should go."

* * *

Marianne saw Jeremy glance toward his shop as they walked through the door to their building. The stroll home had been silent. She didn't know how to approach this rigid stranger. Such a contrast to the companionship of the rest of the day. She thought about the man at the café but felt she could not ask Jeremy about him. With a set face, he turned her toward her side of the building as they entered.

He lit a lantern and handed it to her.

"You go ahead to the lodgings. I'm going to pull out

your trunk from under the worktable and stoke the fire in this stove. I'll join you in a few minutes."

She turned. Shadows elongated on the walls, and she shuddered. What had she gotten herself involved in, and why wouldn't Jeremy tell her? In the living quarters, she went to her area to take her hat and coat off. She tossed them onto the bed and stared at them. She picked up the hat and pulled a long jeweled pin from it and replaced it again. The gentle Jeremy at the lake made her shiver pleasantly. The harsh Jeremy that brought her home made her shiver.

Who was he, and when would she find out? Would she like him?

Dropping the hat again, she picked up the light and went straight back through the sitting room, kitchen, and into her shop. It was decidedly warmer.

Their plan was to start setting her shop up tonight. Just enough to get her launched. Christmas was coming on speedy wings, and she had an idea ladies wanted to shop. And she had brought some new items from the East she was sure would sell.

Only she had thought it would be fun to do this with Jeremy tonight. Now she wasn't sure.

When she arrived, he opened the trunk with a flourish and swept his arm toward it. "Let your boutique commence and be declared open tomorrow," he declared with a smile.

She stared at him. A few hours ago, she would have accepted his performance with a laugh. Now she couldn't quite see his face. How could he change like that?

"Thank you. I will get to work." She stepped forward, set the lantern on the workbench, and pulled things out of the trunk and laid them out. "I appreciate you warming the space and getting my trunk out, Jeremy."

His smile faded and he nodded, then paced around her toward his own workroom.

"I'm going to make a stool for you. It will make your labor back here easier. I'll have it for you tomorrow morning. Nothing fancy. Just a quick fix for now."

And still, he was thoughtful. She watched him limp up to the front and turn the corner.

* * *

He hadn't meant to drop his attitude on Marianne. It was the last thing he wanted to do. But Ambrose Kircher seemed to be shadowing him, and it unnerved him. What could the fellow hope to achieve? The past could not be changed. And Jeremy had been innocent. Yet Kircher had a grudge against him.

If it was only him, that would be one thing. But now Jeremy had a wife to protect. If Kircher hurt her . . . Jeremy slapped a spindly leg on top of wooden seat and hammered it on. Then another.

He heard shouting and some thumps outside. Something hit the front of his building. Again? Jeremy dropped his hammer and rushed to the door in time to see Kircher raising his fists and shouting insults against Jeremy.

"It was his fault! He shoulda made sure Aichen was out first! I'll get him!"

Sheriff Goodwin pulled Kircher's arms behind him and cuffed him. "Come on, fella. You can't be shouting in the street at night. Let's go and you can sleep it off."

Jeremy slumped against the door, watched the sheriff march Kircher, still yelling, up the street to the jail. When they turned the corner, Jeremy stared at his hands before clenching them against his sides. He closed his eyes.

Lord. What would you have me do? I need your help to figure this out. Help me to protect Marianne. Was I wrong to send for her? But now she's here and I'm discovering how necessary she is to me. This, too, Lord—I don't want to pray for Ambrose Kircher, but please help him.

This made the second night in a row that Kircher had been bellowing in the night in front of Jeremy's shop. Or was it the third?

Seven

Marianne thought the daylight hours would reduce her anxiety from the night before. Things were supposed to look better in the morning, right? But as she scanned her shop and its contents strewn about, all she could think of was the disturbance outside in the street last night. And the night before —her wedding night, no less.

She put her hands on her waist, arms akimbo. She'd seen the worry in Jeremy's eyes last night before he'd masked it. He didn't want her to know whatever it was.

She had heard the shouts, the bumps, and rushed to see. Jeremy had already been at the door. She heard the words bellowed by the man. The same man from the café. What had he accused Jeremy of doing? And who was Aichen? And was his inebriated condition the only reason the sheriff hauled him off to the jail?

She sighed. Last night was supposed to have been an enjoyable time in their shops after the lovely day they had shared. Instead, a strain had existed between them after she had asked her questions and Jeremy had brushed them off.

If he was in some kind of trouble, and it seemed he might be, then it would be her problem too. They were married. Of course it would.

Several times, as they lay in their partitioned room, Marianne had opened her mouth to approach the unknown issues. She knew Jeremy was not sleeping. No snoring came from his side. His knees must have been giving him pain. She'd heard him moving about, and then he'd risen rose and left the room. She knew because she'd heard the pounding in his shop before she finally fell asleep.

Today she would insist on an explanation. If Jeremy had one.

For now, she needed to get this business set up and ready. Clients would be coming in anytime. She wanted the parlor to be ready and the hats, hatpins, gloves, fans, and other items to be on display as fast as she could get them out. She even had jeweled broaches to fasten jackets or adorn hats. She glanced at the empty glass display case and turned back to the work area. The curtain was still pulled back so she could see out the big window.

Really, Jeremy had done a wonderful job for her.

She pulled her hat forms from the trunk and set them on the workbench. She dropped undecorated hats on top of them. Felt, wool, velvet for Christmas. She smoothed out silk, thinking how soft that would make the linings.

Then, hands full of ribbons and other fluffy decorations for hats, she faced the wall, suddenly so grateful for her foresight in learning a trade after her father had passed. It had been a social step down, but so much more satisfying than sitting with embroidery on her lap and enduring piteous glances from former friends.

She focused again on the cube shelves mounted on the

wall above the racks that Jeremy had made for her notions and tools.

Jeremy was everywhere. She had entered his world, after all. Of course she saw his handiwork every place she looked. He had done it for her. She shook her head. He was a study in contrasts. Secrets and generosity.

She shook her head and loaded supplies onto the shelves.

She glanced up when she heard the front door open and saw Sheriff Goodwin head over to Jeremy's side. The hammering stopped, and she heard the rumble of their voices.

* * *

"How did you know who destroyed my shop the other night?"

"I checked on the saloon and overheard Ambrose Kircher boasting about trashing your shop while the town was at the wedding. Did you have any idea?" Sheriff Amos Goodwin's eyes seemed to penetrate Jeremy's skull.

Silence.

"Yeah, I did."

"Why didn't you report it, then?"

"I had no proof."

"Well, now we have a confession with witnesses. Do you want to press charges now?"

Jeremy turned away from the lawman. He wanted an end to this persecution. What else could he call it? He swung back around to face the sheriff.

"The Kircher brothers were my friends. How can I put one of them in jail when the other is dead?"

"Jeremy, Ambrose Kircher is not your friend. He is

doing you harm and will do more. Do you want to rethink this?"

"You're right, Amos." Jeremy shook his head in resignation. "I will press charges against him for destroying my shop. I'll come by the courthouse this afternoon."

"I'm sorry, Jeremy. I know you had good times in the past, but that is over now. Kircher is not the same man he was then. And you can't carry guilt for something beyond your control. Yes, come by the courthouse this afternoon and we'll get it done. Maybe get him put away for a while and give you and your bride a chance to move on." Amos Goodwin winked.

Jeremy grinned back. "You and me both, right?"

"Right." Sheriff Goodwin left the shop.

Jeremy picked up his stick and set it back down. He sat on an unfinished bureau. Ambrose had not destroyed that, at least, just scarred it in places. Jeremy could rub that out. Absently, he rubbed his hand across one of the scars and stared at the floor.

He remembered the good times with the Kircher brothers during his logging days. The joking, back slapping, and beer-drinking contests they had during time off. Teasing among falling trees.

That was before one fell and killed Aichen Kircher and took out Jeremy's knees. Then it all changed. Especially Ambrose Kircher.

Did Ambrose feel betrayed? How? Possibly because Jeremy was able to recover and reclaim his life, when Aichen could not? Could the arrival of Jeremy's bride have snapped something in Ambrose?

What does it take to turn a man against his friends?

* * *

Marianne had to strain to hear the sheriff's words. She had heard bits and pieces and didn't quite know how they went together. Was Jeremy guilty of something? Evidently this Ambrose Kircher thought so. She had to hear the story from Jeremy. It might be important to her.

She heard feminine laughter behind her and whirled around just in time to direct Minerva and Helen Dawes into her shop. That was close. She didn't want Jeremy to know she'd been eavesdropping. For now, she had clients. She hoped.

As she directed the ladies forward, she saw Sheriff Goodwin leave.

"You see this space at the front. I noticed it the other day when we were here. Chairs, maybe a soft sofa—"

"Really, Helen. A sofa? This is a business, not a parlor." Minerva cut her off as she paced across the window and scrutinized the walls. "I should think striped wallpaper."

"I . . . uh . . ."

"Now, ladies. Of course this is a business, but striped wallpaper would really be too stark. I would suggest deep red roses," Mrs. Beck reached up to straighten her hat, which had slipped to the back of her head.

Minerva Dawes faced Marianne. "We have come to whisk you off to the mercantile. Get your hat and coat."

"Well, um—"

"We are here to help you decorate your shop, dear." Mrs. Beck glared at Minerva, smiled sweetly at Marianne, and tapped her shoulder lightly.

"Just advice, dear Marianne. We don't want to overwhelm you." Helen Dawes glanced around as she spoke. "Rugs too," she muttered.

Marianne looked from one to the other. She wasn't going to be heard, so she sighed and surrendered. She fled to her room for a quick deep breath as she pinned on her hat. Then she grabbed her coat and reticule and rejoined the ladies.

As she was ushered out of her own shop by the Busy Bees, Marianne rolled her eyes at Jeremy in passing. When he flashed a knowing grin, she stuck her tongue out at him. The sound of his laughter followed her out the door.

"I hope you can find just what you need. If not, Phineas Prentiss has those nice catalogs," Helen Dawes said as they hustled across the street.

"Montgomery Ward, Helen. I keep telling you that," Minerva retorted.

Marianne put her head down against the icy wind that whipped around them. One hand held her hat secure, and she peeked up to see the ladies struggling with their hats too. She wanted to laugh at Mrs. Beck, who nearly lost her hat, then slapped it back on with a determined purse to her lips. Marianne might have to put some thought into how she could make wearing a hat easier for this hapless lady.

At last they reached the door. Marianne would have stood back and waited for the other ladies to file in, but they pushed her forward and squeezed through the door after her.

Oh dear, what kind of day was this going to be?

Shopping was necessary—she needed so much to start her business. But as much as the ladies might rush her, she would go slowly. She did not intend to impose on Jeremy financially any more than she had to. She thought he might struggle some himself after the disastrous assault on his shop.

Marianne stopped to survey her surroundings. The

ladies all disappeared into the long, cavernous structure. Lanterns hung at intervals from the ceiling. She wondered how they were lit every day. Counters and shelves lined the walls, and food bins stood in the middle. Canned goods stacked up in both places. She saw colorful candy jars fixed behind the cash register, and smiled. Perhaps those had to be kept away from wandering hands. Fabric bolts, notions, and some ready-made clothing filled a front corner. Probably so colors and threads could be examined in daylight.

She noted the Christmas trappings and thought she might come back for decorations for her shop. Toys were set close to the fabric area. Marianne thought that might be designed to catch the eyes of mamas. Dolls sat in prams, jack-in-the-boxes along the floor.

Marianne wandered through the goods. She heard the chatter from the Busy Bees as well as other patrons who stood before displays or held up articles of clothing. Some ladies collected spools of thread and lace.

"There is some lovely brocade over here that would go well on chairs. Is Louisa McNeil going to upholster for you?" Mrs. Beck indicated the area to Marianne, and she followed her.

Before long she was directed to wallpaper and paint. Then to the catalogs, until her head was spinning.

"Can I help, Mrs. Stafford?" Suddenly Mr. Prentiss was before her, his apron flapping.

"Soon, sir. But I think not today." Marianne saw the expectant faces out the corner of her eye. She stood straighter. She would make her own decisions. She looked at the man. "But I will be back soon, ready to order."

* * *

Jeremy finished signing papers. He laid down the pen and pushed them toward the clerk. A weight had dropped on his shoulders when he had been informed that Ambrose Kircher had been released early this morning. Apparently they couldn't hold him once the effects of drink had passed. Now that charges had been filed, the law would be looking for Kircher. How would that help Jeremy? Kircher knew the area well.

Jeremy leaned on his stick as he exited around the balustrade spindles and out the door to the stairs. In frustration he thumped his stick on each rung as he stepped to the ground. That stick served more than one purpose. The wind battered him, and he pushed his hat more tightly onto his head. He paused to look down the street.

People hurried back and forth getting tasks finished. Probably before the heavily laden clouds unloaded the threatening sleet. The Beck Bank doors flew open and closed regularly. A group of men stood at the Hanford Mining Office. He looked across to the quiet hotel. A supply barge was due to port soon—he'd seen it idling in the river before it slipped to the dock. Seagulls flew overhead, calling to one another, and he heard the river churning. The hotel would not be quiet for long.

As he passed Betty's Café, the smell of cooking beef wafted by his nose. Must be lunch. His stomach growled. The Oldenburg Tailor shop looked quiet enough. Glancing in the window, he saw a young woman working. He frowned. He didn't remember the old man hiring anyone. But wasn't one of the new brides a seamstress? Whose bride? Oh yes, Deputy Garrison. Jeremy grinned at the thought of his sassy young daughter. A new wife might be just what he needed for that girl of his.

Colorful skirts poked out the door of the mercantile and whipped around. Ladies held them down. Jeremy smiled and wondered how Marianne had coped with the Busy Bees.

The smile dropped from his face as he looked toward his own and Marianne's shops. Beyond them lay open fields and trees. Could he be any more vulnerable?

"What's got you tied up in knots?"

Jeremy started as Thad came up behind him. A warning to him to be more aware. On guard from now on.

"Just looking at the fields beyond my shop."

Thad looked. "So?"

"I learned that Kircher is free after a night in jail. Guess drinking isn't enough to keep him there."

"You haven't said anything about Kircher being responsible for trashing your shop. Has anything changed?"

"I just came from the courthouse to press charges against him. Sheriff Goodwin came by this morning to say that he heard Kircher brag about it at the tavern."

"Man, I'm sorry. What are you going to do?"

They arrived at the carpentry shop, and Jeremy let them in. He pursed his lips and tossed his stick to a corner.

"I don't know yet. But I have to keep Marianne safe."

Her beautiful face flashed before him, and he glanced at the mercantile. A pain seized his chest as he thought of her in danger. He nearly flung his hand over it. Would she see him as a man to trust? If he had to fight for her, he would. But with his bum knees, would he be enough to protect her?

Eight

Marianne parted with the ladies at the door of the mercantile. The wind continued to whip around them, and they all shivered in unison.

"I think it's time to mosey on home now, Marianne," Mrs. Beck declared, holding on to her hat with one hand and her skirt with another. "We'll be back to help decorate your shop when you are ready."

"Indeed yes," agreed Minerva Dawes as Helen nodded. "With so much to look at today, it's a wonder you aren't ready to order. But we will check back with you often."

The ladies really were dears, and they meant well, but their company went a long way. Marianne thanked them and breathed a sigh of relief as she trekked back home.

Home? The thought surprised her. Jeremy's form appeared in her mind.

She shook her head and entered her shop and paused. Mrs. McNeil and Amelia stood by her glass case. A Christmas wreath lay on the top.

"I hope it is all right that I brought the wreath. I mean it to be a housewarming and Christmas gift it to you. The doors on the other shops have one, and I thought you might like one too." Mrs. McNeil gently fingered the white, blue, and gold glittery pine bough. "It's a little different than the others, but I thought it looked more like you when I saw it."

"Oh my. I love it. Thank you for your thoughtfulness. I will have Jeremy hang it this afternoon." Marianne examined the wreath, then removed her coat and dropped her reticule on her worktable. "It's beautiful, Mrs. McNeil."

"You are very welcome, my dear. I hope you will consider us family, like Jeremy does."

Marianne looked up at the kind face, and her heart warmed. "I would love that."

"Well, we are on our way home before it gets much darker outdoors. Thad is with Jeremy in his shop, and we waited for you here." Mrs. McNeil embraced her and walked to the connecting foyer.

Amelia McNeil wandered the empty space by the window. Though the light coming in was dim, it still outlined her youthful figure as she turned toward Marianne. "You'll get used to the Busy Bees. They mean well and want the best for the town and its citizens."

"I believe that."

"Greetings, Marianne. It's good to see you again. I am collecting my ma and sister. Time to go home." Thad McNeil entered the shop, with Jeremy just behind him.

"Yes indeed." Mrs. McNeil tightened her gloves and picked up a reticule. "I'm sure our neighbors will be happy to see us as well as our livestock. Marianne, I will be in touch about upholstering your chairs when Jeremy has them ready. Just send a message to me."

"Thank you—I will."

Jeremy and Marianne stood together at the door as their

friends left. Along with the relief of quiet, Marianne became aware of a sudden tension filling the room. Was it her? Or was it him?

Would Jeremy finally tell her what was happening?

* * *

Alone with his bride.

The presence of this lovely, charming woman beside him scrambled his brain. One glance at her rosy lips put a longing inside that pushed everything else outside. He pulled his eyes away from her.

The trouble was, as soon as he stopped looking, the thoughts and actions of the day crowded in, and that was not much better. He felt the weight of keeping her safe. At the same time, guilt filled him for putting her in this situation. But how could he have known he would be bringing her into danger?

And even if he did, how could he not bring her?

I can't help falling in love with you.

"I see that I will have to decorate this place for Christmas." Marianne moved to the window, then to a side wall. "I think I will need some hooks. Can you do that for me?"

He had whiplash. He jerked his head sideways and back. Why hadn't he thought about more Christmas decorations? He had been so caught up in preparing for Marianne, he'd barely considered Christmas décor for her shop.

"The wreath that the McNeils brought over today is beautiful," she continued.

Wreath? What wreath?

He must have looked puzzled, because she laughed and walked to the glass counter to pick up a wreath.

"Oh, *that* wreath."

"Yes, the one you just now noticed was here only because I picked it up to show you." She sounded exasperated, but the amusement in her eyes gave her away. He relaxed and grinned.

"Well, uh, I admit that I'm not too aware of such things."

"Yes, I can see that will fall to me."

"Do you mind?" He peered more closely at her.

She had held the wreath up by the door but turned at his question. "No, Jeremy, of course I don't mind. Decorating is an enjoyable task. But if you would put a nail in this new door of ours, I will hang this wreath there to welcome our customers. I'm sure even men will feel it's touch as they enter." She smiled, still holding the ornament and not leaving the doorway.

"Oh. You mean now."

"Yes, now."

"Let me get my hammer and a nail, then." He hobbled into his shop, barely brushing by her as he did. Along with the sizzle that raced up the arm that touched her, shame at his halting steps dogged him. Would she be able to look beyond his permanently injured knees?

He heard her draw in her breath. He wanted to think she was affected by him like he was by her, but more likely, she was just worried that he might fall.

He grabbed his tools and she stepped aside for him to open the door. Immediately the cold barreled in.

"Hurry, Jeremy. We don't want to heat the outdoors or let it steal our warmth." She held out the wreath to him, and he hung it on the nail. "Let me grab my wrap. I want to go out and see how it looks." She flung her outer garment over her shoulders and rushed out the door and into the street.

"Close the door," she instructed, and he stepped out and obeyed. She tipped her head, looked up the street and back, nodded. "Yes, ours is definitely the prettiest one. Bless Mrs. McNeil."

He was still standing there as she hurried back up onto the boardwalk and stumbled.

Right into his arms.

Right where he wanted her to be.

She wrapped her arms around him, and he steadied her. When she looked up, he couldn't help it. He lowered his head, and her eyes closed. Her sweet lips were soft under his, and heat blazed up through him. He tightened his arms.

He could have stayed that way the rest of the day.

But she wriggled. He let her go.

Her eyes were wide this time. And she slid by him.

"It's cold out here. Let's go inside."

Should he apologize? But no. She was his wife.

"Thank you, Jeremy, for hanging the wreath. It's a start for us this holiday season." She hung her wrap on the coat rack he'd placed by her inner door earlier that day. "It's close to dinnertime. Perhaps we should see what is left from what the town provided for us this week."

Without looking at him, she marched back to the living quarters.

He limped along behind her, still wondering if he'd made a mistake. He stopped to put more wood into her shop stove before entering the living quarters.

She was already setting food on the table from the icebox. She filled plates to set in the warming oven. He moved to the cookstove and shoved more wood into that too.

"Is there anything I can do to help?"

She indicated the nearly whistling teakettle on the cookstove and a teapot next to it. "You can make tea. The ham, beans, and potatoes are warming up now. I'm nearly finished slicing this bread. As soon as the tea is done and the food on the table, we can eat."

Soon they sat down to their meal. As Marianne put her napkin in her lap, Jeremy held out his hand. She looked over at him and placed her hand in his. He bowed his head and closed his eyes to pray. Now that they were actually sitting down to a meal as a married couple, he meant to start on the right foot.

"Thank you, Almighty God, for this day and the gifts you have given. We dedicate this home, this marriage, and this meal to you. Amen."

Was that enough? He felt a rightness in it and knew that God had accepted his words. When he opened his eyes, Marianne's were on him. She quickly let go of his hand and poured tea into both cups.

After a few bites, he cleared his throat. "I'm sorry that in the rush of everything the last few days, no, week. I never thought much about Christmas."

"That's all right." She sipped her tea and picked up her fork and knife to daintily cut a slice of meat. "I think I can manage to take care of that. My business isn't up and running yet."

"As to that, your chairs are close to being finished. Thad put in a few hours this week. I don't really know what else you might want. But if you know, I'll put it on priority and mostly have your shop furnished by Christmas. There is always the Montgomery Ward catalog to order from, too, though anything you order won't be here for a few weeks."

"Thank you. I appreciate that. You can see, as you walk through my shop, that I have already worked on emptying my trunk. So I do have some items to work with."

"When do you plan to have your door open for business?"

"Tomorrow if I have customers. They just won't have a place to sit yet. But so far, everyone is very understanding, even with Christmas a week away."

A silence fell as they ate.

Jeremy cleared his throat. She looked at him expectantly.

"Thank you for putting the meal together. I was hungry." He stood to clear his plate.

She nodded and returned her gaze to her own plate.

"I'll help with cleanup, of course," he tossed over his shoulder as he moved toward the heating water on the side of the cookstove.

"Thank you." She joined him and grabbed a knife, which she stabbed into the soap bar and swished around for suds.

"I think I'll wait for a minute," he joked, and backed away with his hands up.

"Suit yourself."

Uh-oh. What had he done?

"Are you upset with me?"

"No, of course not. Why would I be upset?"

"Okay, then." He wasn't going to get anywhere with this. "I'll finish clearing the table and put things away."

"Fine. That's a good idea."

The truth was that he wanted to clear the air about that kiss. How should he go about that?

* * *

Marianne knew she was behaving like a spoiled brat, but she couldn't seem to stop herself. First, there was that kiss. His mustache had tickled her mouth. She was embarrassed at how she had swooned in Jeremy's arms. She hardly knew him.

But he was her husband.

Had she laid down any ground rules going into this marriage? What did he expect from her? She couldn't . . . do that. At least, not yet. Still, that kiss left her feeling like jelly even now. She scrubbed a bowl hard, and some of the water sloshed over the side. Too bad. She would just have to mop it up later.

And then Jeremy was wiping it up. She softened, momentarily.

But what had he been about to say at the table that he didn't say?

And then, what about the mystery man who seemed to be angry with Jeremy? He had not offered any kind of explanation. Shouldn't she know?

She was his wife.

The kitchen was cleaned up and the last dish washed, when Jeremy limped into the sitting room and lit the lamps. Light revealed the two comfortable chairs and the table between them. A rug covered the floor. It was bare essentials. But a curtain covered a back window. Marianne's gaze swept over the room, mentally thinking of changes she could make so this would be home.

He settled into one of the chairs and picked up a book from the table.

She sat in the other chair, her hands uncomfortably empty. "You like to read?"

"You sound like that surprises you. Why?"

"I don't know. I suppose because you live in the Wild West, or something silly like that. What is it you are reading?"

"It's a novel by Jules Verne, *Mathias Sandorf*. This author writes adventure, intrigue, and revenge. Jules Verne and Mark Twain kept me well entertained as I recuperated last year." He held up the orange book with its detailed drawings.

"It certainly has a colorful cover. I see you have other books in the bookcase. May I look?"

Now *he* looked surprised. "Of course. This is your home now. Read whatever you like."

Now she felt ridiculous. "Jeremy, we need to talk."

He blinked and tensed. He set the book back on the table.

"It's the first opportunity we've had to talk about anything," she began, threading and unthreading her fingers.

"A lot has happened this week," he agreed. "About that kiss—I'm sorry to have made you uncomfortable."

She waited, but he didn't say anything else. Why would she expect anything else? She felt the blush rising up her neck. He should be the gentleman and initiate this conversation. She took a breath to begin, but then he leaned forward, his elbows on his knees.

"I know I didn't ask. But you are beautiful, and I just couldn't help myself. I don't want you to be uneasy with our, uh, marriage arrangement. We haven't discussed how to forge ahead."

She relaxed. He understood. She should have known. He'd been kind and considerate in most everything. Well, except that first day when he'd railroaded her into this marriage. Still, she argued with herself, she had agreed to come on his dime.

"Thank you."

"I don't intend to push anything, just so you know." He looked so earnest.

"It would be good to just get to know each other for now, don't you think?"

"I do." He smiled and held out a hand.

She smiled back and put her hand into his, and he drew it to his lips and kissed it, his eyes on hers, just as he had done at their wedding. She couldn't breathe or look away. How could he do this already?

"A seal and a promise."

Oh.

"A seal and a promise," she repeated.

He settled back in his chair. But she wasn't finished.

"Jeremy."

He tensed again. "Yes?"

"Who is Ambrose Kircher?"

He went silent, and she thought he would ignore the question.

"Why do you ask?"

"Is he responsible for wrecking your shop?"

"It looks that way." He sighed, picking up his book again.

But she would not be dismissed. "Did I hear the sheriff ask you to press charges?"

"You did." He watched her now. Answering her questions but not volunteering any other information.

"And will you?"

"I already have. Now don't worry about him anymore. The sheriff has all the information, and he will take care of the situation."

"What situation?"

Jeremy stiffened. "Marianne, it's taken care of. I don't want you to worry. You are safe."

They stared at each other. She wasn't going to get any further tonight.

A short time later she lay in her bed in the dark, staring at the ceiling. She had thought Jeremy would slip into his side of the room after she had settled in. After only a few short nights, it bothered her that he wasn't on the other side of the partition. Jeremy was worried about this Ambrose Kircher. She wished he would tell her the truth. Now she lay listening to the hammering in his shop.

She put her fingers to her lips.

* * *

Gratitude. That was what Jeremy felt. His bride was safe and sound just beyond the wall, and so far the evening was quiet. No yelling, bumping, or knocking. Maybe Ambrose Kircher had sense enough not to show up around town for a while. If ever, Jeremy hoped.

He swung the hammer that finished connecting legs to the wooden manger. He had planned on this surprise for his bride for Christmas, but decorations just didn't occur to him. Maybe they should have.

This crib would hold the Christ child, which had taken several days to carve before Marianne had arrived. These two pieces were the first of various figures he hoped she would like enough to group in the corner of her shop every Christmas—the only thought he'd given to Christmas décor for her business.

He would show it to her soon and hoped her lovely eyes would light up when she saw it. He wondered if this came under the "decorations" category. Perhaps she would help to design the rest of the figures. Every year he hoped to add another piece. Like starting a family tradition. He liked the idea of that.

Legacy.

Thank you, Lord, for keeping this project safe from Ambrose's rage.

He put away the hammer and recovered the manger in the shadows before he sat down with the Christ figure to finish crafting it. This represented his Savior. It had to be perfect.

He made sure the overhead lamp was directly above and another positioned close on his workbench. Carving was a talent he had discovered during his convalescence. It relaxed him, and when the art revealed itself with every slice of his knife, satisfaction filled his soul.

He worked for a while, his mind drifting. When it wandered to how soft his bride's lips felt under his just hours ago, he nearly cut his thumb. Clutching the figure in one hand, he rested the other on his knee and stared at the wall.

The wall disappeared as her luminescent blue eyes gazed at him. He was sure he'd seen desire in them before the startled expression took over and she'd darted away. He had wanted to smooth the strands of her silky dark hair that the wind had blown free. Even though a near accident propelled her into his arms, he didn't care as long as he could hold her.

His heart yearned. One of these days, he was sure she would be there by choice.

Nine

By Friday Marianne had her shop tools and merchandise set up. Snow had blown in all day on Thursday, so few people had been out in the town. Marianne had bustled around setting things in place. She felt good about it, even if she didn't have furniture or rugs in place yet.

Jeremy had fashioned a curtain rod for her front window, and maybe today or tomorrow she would wander to the mercantile to order a curtain and matching rug. She would have to pick out something that would go well with the material Louisa McNeil had presented her with for the chairs.

Mrs. McNeil had sent, via her son, a variety of fabrics to choose from. Marianne had picked out an elegant blue-and-silver brocade pattern of roses. It was at once tasteful and restful, and Marianne hoped it would lull ladies to linger.

Her glass case gleamed, and its shelves filled with items ladies needed to accessorize their ensembles. Her hat blocks didn't offer much yet, since she had not had time to trim hats. She would get started on that right away. Jeremy had offered to make her more hat blocks for display and working processes. She would need a few different shapes, as ladies often ordered custom hats.

She sidestepped so she could see behind the curtain to her workspace. She hummed with satisfaction as she noted her materials and tools were all in place and ready for use. She would make a new order tomorrow for more to be shipped, since she expected most of her materials would be gone quickly. Christmas was already less than a week away. She would have to work hard to fill demands for Christmas hats.

Ella Weaver, one of her bride companions, had urgently requested a new hat. It seemed that Deputy Sheriff Garrison's twelve-year-old daughter was in need of a new wardrobe. Marianne would get started on this one right away. She mused about the girl as she stared at the empty hat on the block. This was the little girl who had tossed the dead mouse at church during the one and only church service that Marianne had so far attended. She laughed out loud as she remembered the stir that had caused.

"What's so funny?"

She jumped at the voice close to her ear. How had she not heard him coming? She turned to see the gold, green, and brown flecks of his eyes close to hers. So close. As she stared, they softened from amusement to something unnamed that she felt to her toes. His eyes darted from her eyes to her mouth and back. So quickly she would have missed it. Except that she could not tear away her gaze.

She cleared her throat and stepped back. Only a half step. Her body didn't seem inclined to go far. Still, he took his cue and swung from her to look around her shop. She let out a breath.

"I was just thinking of the deputy's little girl and the hat

Ella wants me to make for her." Marianne's words rushed out. "And I remembered the dead mouse she pulled out of her pocket at church last Sunday."

He laughed. Was it slightly forced?

"Yeah, she's a minx, all right. He has his hands full with her."

"Maybe . . . maybe Ella can help him with her."

"I'm sure he would be grateful for all the help he can get."

In the awkwardness of the moment, the Dawes ladies bustled into the shop, both talking at once. Marianne saw Jeremy mask dismay before he turned to them with a welcoming smile.

What might have happened?

"Greetings, ladies. I hope you are staying as dry as possible after our snow yesterday. The streets look a bit slushy, I see."

"Oh my, yes, Mr. Stafford. They are." Helen Dawes gripped her coat with a short shake as they stood in the doorway. Her eyes darted around the shop. "Your shop is coming along nicely, Marianne."

"I should say so." Minerva Dawes strolled in and perused the gloves, fans, broaches, and other niceties laid out in the glass case. "Hmm. I see I need to add a few things to my wardrobe."

Marianne stepped forward, and Jeremy quietly limped back into his own shop. If she weren't still trembling at the might-have-been, she could laugh at his sneaking away.

"But that's not why we are here." Helen came forward and elbowed Minerva.

"It's not?" Marianne shot a bewildered look between them.

"It's not." Minerva sighed and continued to study the merchandise. "We have come to whisk you away."

"What?"

"Yes indeed," Helen exclaimed. "Some of us have decided that the town is drab in this winter season. But Christmas should be bright and cheerful. When the snow kept us inside yesterday, we decided to do something about it."

"So we are going to decorate potted trees and have some of these big, strapping men hanging around town haul them to the street corners." Minerva took up the explanation. "Wreaths on the doors are all well and good, but decorated trees on the corners help the Christmas spirit along."

Marianne wondered what this had to do with her.

"We've come to fetch you. At the hotel, we need all the hands we can use. Christmas is just next week," Helen said.

"And we must have the trees decorated and arranged on the streets right away," Minerva added, still looking in the glass case. "I will come back," she muttered.

Oh. Marianne looked around. She supposed her shop was at a place where she could take a break. And if her customers were all going to be decorating and placing trees, she might as well join them.

* * *

Jeremy had drawn a shaky breath when the Dawes ladies had interrupted the moment with his wife. He'd nearly kissed Marianne for the second time. If the Dawes ladies had not walked in when they did, he would have done it. And done it well.

What might have happened?

He would never know now.

He heard their conversation and thought about it. He had been concerned for Marianne's safety, as Kircher had not yet been arrested. Jeremy had considered many excuses as to why she should not be outside of the building alone. But that bordered on paranoia, and she was a grown woman, after all.

Maybe Marianne would be safe enough with all the ladies around her. How could he extract a promise from her to stay with them without arousing her suspicion?

Trust Me, son.

I know, Lord. I'm trying. Why is it harder to trust her welfare to You than my own?

He knew. It had to do with faith. But maybe his faith just couldn't stretch that far?

What was wrong with him?

God had pulled him through so much over the last couple of years. The accident had stopped him in his tracks, all right. Not only could he not walk for months, but God had parked him spiritually too. The drinking and barroom weekends had halted like the wheels on a wagon going downhill when the brake was applied. For weeks he'd lain still, his knees unable to hold him. Doc Paine had done his best, but some things just had to heal on their own.

If it had not been for the McNeil family, only God knew what would have become of him.

"Jeremy?"

He straightened from his project, dropping the hammer to his side. The hanging lamps swayed slightly as the Dawes ladies opened the outside door. His lovely wife poked her head around the corner. Though a chill zipped through the room, he only felt the heat of his body flushing through him at the sight of her. He was going after that kiss tonight!

"Yes? I heard you talking. I suspect you are going along to the hotel now for the rest of the afternoon?"

"You suspect rightly." She laughed. "I'll be home in time for dinner."

With that, she disappeared, and the quiet was too much. He barely bit back the words he wanted to say.

Be careful.

Watch out around you.

Don't go anywhere by yourself.

She would not have taken that well.

Jeremy leaned against the wall. Did he need to be so antsy? Or had he built up the danger in his mind? And why was Kircher so bent on causing trouble? Still, there had been no new episodes with Kircher for several days. Maybe he had fled the area, since he would be pressed into jail if he came around. Jeremy's charges still stood.

When had his friend become his enemy?

Jeremy rubbed a hand across his forehead, then down the side of his face. What had he done to Ambrose?

He lost his only family during that accident.

But how did the Kircher family involve Jeremy? He had tried to save Aichen Kircher. He was the closest to him when the tree fell but just couldn't get to him in time. Jeremy had nearly lost his own life. Certainly his life had changed because his knees had been crushed.

His thoughts kept pinging back and forth. He wished he could land somewhere and think a thing out, but it just jumbled up in his mind.

He was falling in love with Marianne. But he couldn't tell her. She had not even been in town for a full week yet, even if they had been married for most of it. How could his feelings have ballooned so fast? Maybe he had begun to long for her through her sweet letters.

I can't help falling in love with you.

The words just flowed.

He thought maybe she felt something toward him, too. A beginning.

But the shadow of danger hung over them.

* * *

Marianne set the tureen of stew on the table with the last of the bread that she had baked yesterday. Wedding leftovers were long gone. That was too bad. She spent time putting meals together now, but at least her shop was just steps away.

"Come sit down," she called to Jeremy. He was fiddling with another lamp table in the sitting room. Having another would be helpful with both their evening pursuits.

He pulled out a chair to seat her first. With a blush, she sat. He insisted on acting as the gentleman. She was glad she had gone through with this mail order marriage.

Jeremy held out his hand, waiting for her to place hers on it. He prayed for their dinner. Yes, she had made the right decision. A man who prayed was one who could be trusted.

He filled a bowl with stew and handed it to her with a smile. She gave him her bowl; he filled it and set it before himself. She blew on her bite to cool it, but Jeremy stuffed his spoonful into his mouth.

"Mm-mm. Good stew," he said after swallowing.

How had he not burned his throat? She stared at him.

"What?"

"Isn't that a bit hot?"

"I like hot."

She filled her own mouth with her cooler portion, her amusement safely hidden.

"How did it go with the ladies today?" Jeremy buttered a piece of bread and took a bite.

Marianne swallowed quickly as a gurgle of laughter escaped her. "Oh fine. You know those ladies. One of them set us to decorating, and another lady made us rearrange them. It happened with several of the trees. We changed garlands on one tree three times until they pronounced it good."

He laughed with her. "And did you get one on every street?"

"Oh yes. The Bees actually went into Betty's Café to recruit men to move the trees. I don't know if they even finished their dinners."

"Poor guys."

"If you peek outside tomorrow, you will see trees all lined up and down the street. And the ones on either side of ours as well. I think Wild Rose Ridge is ready for Christmas."

"Hmm. Did anyone walk you home?" His meal finished, he rose to take his bowl to the water reservoir by the cookstove.

Marianne watched his retreating back. "Why would anyone walk me home?"

"Just asking." He scrubbed his bowl and came for hers.

"Asking why?" She cleared what was left on the table as he swished out her bowl and dried it.

"It gets dark early, and I just want you to be safe."

He set the teakettle on the stove and pulled two mugs from the shelf. She wiped the table and stood to face him.

"All right, Jeremy. I think we both know what's on your

mind, and it's time to talk about it. Shall we take our tea into the sitting room?"

He closed his eyes briefly. "Yes, I suppose it is. I had hoped to protect you from all of this."

She stepped close to him. "Jeremy, you can't. If that man continues to harass you, then I'm involved already. You must know that."

He lifted a hand and smoothed back a strand of hair from her face. She shivered, and he dropped his hand. No, no, she wanted—what?

Jeremy grabbed his stick and limped with the cups into the sitting room to set them on the table between their chairs. Marianne brought the teapot and poured it before she sat down.

"Talk," she ordered, both hands holding her cup in front of her mouth and her eyes on him. She knew he was reluctant, but she was tired of tiptoeing around the subject. And she liked to be prepared. Just in case.

* * *

Where should he start? His wife's expectant eyes bored into him, and he knew she would not let it go until she knew the whole of it. What kind of protector was he? He took a deep breath and dove in.

"You know that Ambrose Kircher's brother, Aichen, was killed in a falling tree accident, right? Well, that's the same accident that crushed my knees. We all saw it coming, even Aichen. He started to run, but it was too late. I ran in and tried to pull him out, but the tree got my knees when it settled. Aichen was crushed, and both my knees were broken." He stared at the wall, reliving that terrible time.

She put down her mug and wrapped her fingers around

his. His stare shifted from the wall to their hands and then to her face. He expected to see pity, but it was compassion that gave him encouragement to continue. He tightened the grip.

"I don't remember much about either of us being extracted. But after an excruciating trip in the back of a wagon, I ended up in Doc Paine's house for a few weeks. My legs were immobilized at first. When he let me move them, I went to the McNeils' for recuperation and recovery. I never saw Aichen again. I didn't see Ambrose for several months either."

He shifted his knees, watching his legs move.

"It was Doc Paine who gave me the idea to whittle. And when he saw what I could do, he suggested that I think about opening a carpentry shop once I could get around again. I resisted. It's too easy to think of yourself as an invalid when you are injured and it will never heal properly. But Thad took up that torch and prodded me. When I still resisted"—he smiled—"Louisa gave me no peace. She didn't mince words either."

"Even with encouragement, it takes bravery to move beyond irreparable damage. I have seen their pride in you. And the way the whole town came to help the day after your shop was ravaged says a lot." She lightly rocked their hands.

"Staying with the McNeils relit the flame of my faith. I'd drifted away from God. I hate the idea that I took Him to the saloon with me. But I am grateful He never left me."

They sat silent for a few minutes.

"I'm so glad that God led me to you, Jeremy," Marianne said softly. So softly that he had to lean in. "I think you might be relighting the flame of my faith. I see Him in you."

Joy flooded his heart until he thought it would burst.

He wanted love, and he still hoped for that. But this was the foundation they could build a marriage upon. He lifted her hand and kissed it.

"That's what you did at our wedding," she murmured.

"What's that?"

"Kissed my hand."

"Always a promise."

"Always a promise."

She waited. Jeremy knew he had to spill it all.

"What I can't understand is why Ambrose is bent on harassment. We were friends—now we are enemies."

"It must hurt."

"It does. He visited me once at McNeils'. He was normal, or what was now normal in his grief. But after some of the things he has yelled this week, I know he blames me for Aichen's death. But I was trying to *save* his brother."

"Maybe he has to blame somebody."

"And I was the last one to be close to Aichen when he was still alive." Jeremy sat back as Marianne nodded. "But there were witnesses everywhere. That's a logger's nightmare. You can't look away. It's like everything slows down. How could Ambrose blame me?" He ended in a whisper, as his throat seemed to close up.

"People think strange things in their grief, Jeremy. Witnesses wouldn't matter." Marianne stroked his arm with her other hand.

"Why now? And not before?"

"Maybe as long as you were suffering, Ambrose could safely lay the blame on you. You weren't going anywhere. But when you started to recuperate, he got angry."

"And when I started to move on, that ignited resentment inside him."

"Yes." She nodded again.

He shifted in his chair. "And when a bride arrived for me, he had to act."

"I'm so sorry, Jeremy. But yes, I think that too. In his mind, if his brother can't live a life, then you shouldn't either."

Her voice hitched, and Jeremy turned to face her. He probed her face and saw her try to hide fear in her deep-blue eyes. This was why he had not wanted to tell her.

"I needed to know," she whispered. "You did right to tell me. Now we will both be prepared."

He brought her hand to his lips again, wishing it was more. He planned to keep the promises he had made to her.

Ten

Marianne hummed as she swept the floor in her shop Saturday morning. Since the snow on Thursday, the sun had peeked out in between clouds. The air was crisp and cold, but the sun streaks through her window warmed her soul.

The shop had already hosted several visitors. Its bare state didn't seem to bother anyone, and Jeremy planned to finish her chairs today. She had ordered her rugs and wallpaper, so it was coming together nicely.

She scooped up the bits of dirt into the dustpan and, with a wry smile, walked outside to dump them. Soon that dirt would make its reappearance in her shop. But one must try to keep cleanliness at the forefront.

After putting away the broom and dustpan, she rolled the curtain back a bit to her workspace. The sweet little hat for Deputy Garrison's daughter hung on a block. The design for it danced in her head, and she was ready to work on it.

She picked up the hat form as the rhythm of bumps emanated from Jeremy's shop. Awareness tingled down her spine. Earlier that morning she had nearly walked in on Jeremy as he changed from his nightshirt to daywear. Her cheeks burned now as she remembered how quickly she had stepped back to wait. But the picture of his strong chest remained in her mind.

Dr. Paine had given Jeremy exercises to do to strengthen his knees, and he faithfully did those, as well as other trainings. He never missed, and already Marianne had learned not to interfere with his morning calisthenics.

"Ah, what have we here? New fribbles for the ladies?" a man drawled as he stepped into her shop.

Marianne stiffened. How dare this man be so condescending? She looked up and shuddered as she recognized the man who had glowered at her several times in the past week. He must be Ambrose Kircher.

The smell of alcohol filled the room and stifled Marianne's breathing. The man's hair hung in uneven strings around his face, and an unruly beard covered his chin. He moved around the window in the empty space where her chairs would go. He must be watching for the sheriff.

Marianne's heart pounded. "May I help you, sir?"

Where was Jeremy?

Her fingers closed around one of her longer hatpins, and she squeezed it in the folds of her skirt. She stayed behind the counter.

The man laughed. It was not a pleasant sound. She carefully set the hat form on the block and spread her feet, just in case.

The man sidestepped closer to her, keeping an eye out the window. So he was distracted—that should help her.

He laughed. "Oh, a pretty thing like you can help me a lot."

He reached for her, and she stuck her pin in his arm.

No way was she losing it. She yanked it back just as quickly and dashed around him.

He howled, stepped back, and slapped a hand to his arm. "You little—"

Jeremy loped in and skidded to a stop, his loose shirt flapping around him, and took in the big man gripping an arm to Jeremy's defiant wife, her hands in the folds of her skirt.

"Kircher! What are you doing here?"

Kircher straightened up, dropping his hand even as blood stained the cloth of his arm. His face changed to contempt as he looked Jeremy up and down. "Figured I would get me some entertainment for the afternoon. A woman wants a man, Stafford. Not some no count cripple. Thought you were expanding your business with one of those mail order lightskirts." He sneered.

"Brides," Jeremy snarled before he bent to take out the man at the knees. Both went down and rolled over. Marianne skirted around them. She worried for Jeremy and meant to call for help. She ran into Sheriff Goodwin as she yanked open the door.

The sheriff strode through the front door. He threw his hands on both men to pull them apart. "Haven't the two of you settled your differences yet?"

Marianne noticed people gathering in front of the millinery window. Why did people have to gather where they weren't wanted?

She reached for Jeremy to help him off the floor, but he shrugged her off. He gripped the side of the counter and hauled himself to his feet, a grimace on his face. He straightened his shirt, then let his hands dangle at his sides. He stood, and she searched his now impassive face.

"Come on, Kircher. You don't belong here." Sheriff

Goodwin pulled the other man up. "I warned you about disturbing the peace and harassment the other night. And there are charges pending against you. You could try to keep yourself out of trouble. Now you're under arrest."

Kircher scowled at Jeremy but said nothing as the sheriff cuffed his hands behind his back. Then the words erupted from him.

* * *

Jeremy winced. The whole town seemed to have gathered outside the window. Just what he needed. An audience.

"My brother should be here! Not you! She should belong to Aichen. He should have had the chance to live. You stole his life. You'll pay, Stafford!"

"Get out." Jeremy growled, gritting his teeth.

There was no point in defending himself. Kircher would continue to blame him. The community already knew what had happened. If he weren't so angry right now, he would roll his eyes at the repeated rhetoric.

"Come on, Kircher. Let's get you out of here." Sheriff Goodwin pushed and shoved the unwilling prisoner in front of him.

"You can't jail me." Kircher tried to fling his cuffed fists at the sheriff.

"Try answering to damaged property with malicious intent, interruption of public services, and aggravating circumstances—like harassment. And watch those cuffs or I'll add assaulting an officer of the law to it. Come on, let's go."

As the sheriff yanked Kircher out, yelling obscenities, the crowd dissipated.

In the sudden quiet, Jeremy relaxed, smoothed his hair

back, and rubbed his knuckles. He looked Marianne up and down.

"I'm sorry for the name calling."

"You didn't do it. You even defended me and the other brides."

"Did he hurt you?"

She shook her head. "No, mostly scared me. I can't stop trembling."

He closed the space between them and slipped his arms around her. She leaned into him. He breathed in her mock orange blossom scent and rested one hand on her head as she dropped it on his shoulder. Somehow her softness soothed his soul. They stood until her trembling stopped.

She backed up, and he let her go. She held up a hatpin with a red tip. No, not a red tip. That had to be Kircher's blood.

Jeremy looked from it to her face. Then he blinked at the pin and laughed.

"Why are you laughing?"

He sobered up and rested against the counter. "Kircher's got a pretty big chip on his shoulder. I thought you might need rescuing, but maybe you had the situation in hand all by yourself."

She sighed heavily and set down the hatpin. "I don't think I would have deterred him for long. Thank you for coming to my rescue."

"You'll do, Marianne Stafford. How about a cup of tea? I think we've earned it."

"That sounds wonderful. Let's add lunch to it."

Her smile sparkled at him. His chest hitched. He held out a hand to her, and she took it.

* * *

After lunch of tea and sandwiches, Marianne swept the floor for the second time that day, glad that she had worn the brown serviceable skirt and the shirtwaist with the flower sprigs. Maybe the dirt wouldn't show on her clothes too much.

After the morning's traffic, she reflected that she should invest in entry rugs for feet wiping. Of course, it wasn't every day that someone stomped into her shop to threaten her. She hoped she would never have to see that man again.

How could Jeremy have been friends with him?

Then again, the man probably had come unhinged after losing his brother.

Still, she hoped she would never encounter him again.

Jeremy went to his shop and intended to work on her chairs. She looked around the empty space in her shop in front of the counter and imagined it furnished. She rested her chin on her hands as she gripped the broom handle. She could see in her mind the wallpaper hung, chairs, table and lamps in place, rugs on the floor, and lace curtains at the window.

"My goodness, Marianne. I see you have already set up shop, even though your décor is not done yet." Mrs. Beck tottered in, and Marianne jumped. "Oh dear, I scared you."

"Oh no, not at all. I was just imagining my shop being put together. Thank you for noticing that I am ready to start business." Marianne noted Mrs. Beck standing a little taller with the compliment. She made a mental note to put bells on the door so she would not be surprised by her customers.

"You certainly have had quite the morning, I understand," Mrs. Beck wandered along the glass case, trailing a finger.

Marianne hoped she wasn't picking up dust on her glove.

"Mercy, with the tailor shop's broken window, Mr. Stafford's shop destroyed, and now the morning events here. All in one week."

"Yes, well, some days are eventful. Have you come to see about a hat?" Marianne wanted to put out a hand to catch Mrs. Beck's hat as the lady nodded. She must have pinned it well, because it looked like it was barely hanging on to the side of her head.

"I need a new hat for Christmas. I fancy you haven't had much time to trim hats, what with so much excitement right after your wedding." She turned to face Marianne.

Marianne studied her client's face, trying to ignore the hanging hat. "I think I can accommodate you, Mrs. Beck. I do have some untrimmed hats in the back. I'm sure we can find one for you."

"Oh yes, do bring them out."

Marianne excused herself and fetched several. Mrs. Beck moved them around, and Marianne steered her in a direction that would flatter her and not overwhelm her head or the eyes of anyone looking at her.

They were discussing several kinds of trims, Marianne trying to restrain Mrs. Beck's extravagance, when she heard the door.

She glanced up to see Elinore Cameron and her mother-in-law with her. As she straightened up to greet her friend, Marianne became aware of Mrs. Beck stiffening.

"Marianne, I'll be in touch about the hat. Use that red and green with the berries on that form there. I must be going, my dear." Mrs. Beck gathered up her reticule and gloves, touched a cheek to Marianne's, nodded to Elinore, and walked out.

Marianne stared after her. What brought on such blatant rudeness?

"Never mind, Marianne. How are you?" Elinore moved closer and embraced Marianne lightly, and Mrs. Cameron made her way to the glass case. Marianne approved of Elinore's new coat—she had come to Wild Rose Ridge with little. It looked like God smiled on her now. Or perhaps her new husband.

"Welcome to my shop, Elinore and Mrs. Cameron." Marianne made sure to include Mrs. Cameron in her welcome. She tried to make up for Mrs. Beck's exit. "It's so good to see you. I've been wondering how you are."

Mrs. Cameron smiled and looked around as Elinore replied. "I have been wondering about you as well. We are taking advantage of the relatively good weather today to come to town and shop."

"Good weather?" Marianne laughed. "Yes, I suppose it is good weather as long as it is not snowing."

"At least we are able to travel. I had to come to see how you are doing with your shop. You must be open for business?"

"Yes, I am. I know I have a long way to go to make this area a pleasant place to shop, but I'm sure that every time you come you will see changes. Do you need Christmas hats?"

"Of course we do."

"Let me move Mrs. Beck's materials, then we can design beautiful hats for both of you."

* * *

"I sold a few hats today." Marianne buttered her bread and set it on the saucer next to her bowl of leftover stew. No one would ever accuse her of being a chef.

Jeremy tried to stretch his legs under the table without her observance. He downed his glass of milk. "I noticed you had a lot of company this afternoon. Did they come in because of curiosity from this morning's activity, or were they really shopping?"

She paused, a spoonful of stew halfway to her mouth, and studied him.

He stared back.

She put her bite into her mouth, chewed, and swallowed. "Do you think I won't draw customers without some fray in my shop?"

"No, of course I don't mean that." Jeremy pushed his bowl aside and sat back. His knees ached, and he knew he would have to do something about it tonight. He didn't want to.

"I'm happy you are on your way to success. I'll soon have the furniture pieces you need. I'll have the chairs ready for Thad to take home for Louisa tomorrow after church. I'm sure it won't take her long to stuff and cover them. You've done well this week."

"Thank you." She inclined her head and took a sip of tea.

He stifled a grunt of pain as he slowly stood and cleared his dishes from the table. Soon he was drying dishes and shelving them as Marianne washed them. The sounds of water swishing and clinking dishes filled the quietness. They had been married now for seven nights, and sometimes he still felt tongue-tied after the evening meal.

Not only that, his knees were killing him. The last thing he wanted to do was to sit and apply another liniment treatment to his knees. He glanced at the bottle on the corner shelf. He had done fairly well all week. But today's brawl with Kircher about did him in. He should have rubbed the liniment on in the shop this afternoon, but he wanted those chairs finished and ready for Thad tomorrow, so he toughed out the pain. Bad plan.

With the last plate put away, he grabbed the bottle of liniment and his stick to help him make it to a chair. Marianne brought mugs and a teapot with her and set it on the table between them.

Jeremy tried not to groan as he lifted a leg to the ottoman. He used his hands to bring the other one up.

"I'm so sorry for the pain," Marianne said softly as she sat on the edge of her seat and faced him. "Is it bad tonight because of the fight this morning? It must be. What can I do to help?"

This was what he didn't want. His bride acting like a nursemaid. He kept his tongue in his mouth until the wave of pain passed. She didn't deserve to be snapped at.

She waited for him to speak, empathy in her eyes.

At least it wasn't pity.

Not looking at her, he rolled his pant legs up to uncover his legs. Well, she was his wife, wasn't she? He didn't hear a gasp.

"I just need to rub this stuff on my knees and hope the pain lessens." He reached for the bottle, but her hand grasped his. Their eyes met.

"Let me do it."

His eyes widened.

"Yes. Please. You are suffering now because you defended me from that awful man today. Let me serve you."

He let go of the bottle, sat back, and closed his eyes. Wife, not nursemaid. "Thank you."

He tried to relax, but the first touch of her hands gently massaging circles into one knee about brought him out of the chair. He forced himself to settle. Her hands were cool and soothing, yet the warmth he felt on his knees wasn't coming only from the bottle. He struggled to control his breathing.

Too soon, she set the cap on the flask and settled back into her own chair.

He opened his eyes to find her staring at him.

"What?"

"Thank you, Jeremy. I'm so glad I came out West to you."

He swallowed, and his voice came out husky. "I'm the one who is blessed."

"I-I think it's time to turn in." She rose.

He stood slowly.

"Jeremy, you didn't have to get up."

He leaned to grab his stick and limped to the stove to bank the fire.

"You're right. It's time to turn in. I thought we might find us a Christmas tree after church tomorrow."

"That sounds lovely. Will you be all right to go?"

Grumpy Jeremy was back. He didn't answer right away. Not until he returned to the sitting room to extinguish the table lamp and light a lantern to lead them to the sleeping quarters.

"I'll be fine after a night's sleep."

"Oh. All right, then."

She turned to the doorway, and Jeremy bumped into her, his knees still not quite steady. She grabbed him around the waist, and somehow the lantern found a surface. Both of Jeremy's arms went around her. Her blue eyes looked like midnight stars as they stared into his. He smoothed her hair back. It felt as silky as he had thought it would. She was warm in his arms.

He hesitated only a moment, but she didn't pull back. Her lips were soft and sweet, and how he had longed to taste them. Again and again.

Her arms tightened around him, and Jeremy's head swam.

His knees threatened to buckle, and he would *not* allow her to become his crutch. Especially not now. He gently unwrapped her arms.

"Time to turn in, sweetheart. You take the lantern."

Eleven

Sweetheart. He had called her sweetheart. And those kisses last night. She had lived them repeatedly most of the night and again when she rose this morning. Marianne squelched a shiver. She had stared at the ceiling a long time after crawling into bed. Something had stirred in her, and she had trembled even as she heard Jeremy move about before all was quiet. They had fallen into a habit of chatting before sleeping. But last night no words were spoken between them.

And now, as they sat together in church, he held her hand. Even through her gloves she could feel the warmth of his fingers. She also felt the warmth crawling up her neck as looks drifted toward her and Jeremy. She held her face straight forward. Let them look. She sat with her husband.

She searched for her bride friends. Elinore sat in the back with her husband and mother-in-law. They had exchanged smiles when Marianne and Jeremy had walked in. Ella sat with Deputy Garrison's family. He had been sent north to sort out some trouble in the mines. Marianne grinned as she remembered the dead mouse from last

Sunday. What would the deputy's little girl have today? Then she frowned and stared in front of her. Was Mr. Kircher secured at the jail?

Other friends scattered around the room. Some sat with their soon-to-be husbands. Miss Val sat in the front row, Preacher Sutton beside her as the first strains of the organ squealed.

Marianne glanced at Jeremy and saw him wince. She stifled a giggle, and he grinned back. Then Minerva Dawes began to screech. A collective shifting of positions moved like a wave through the congregation, and Preacher Sutton stood to invite everyone to join in singing the hymn.

Marianne's mind wandered as Preacher Sutton stepped up to the podium. His voice droned in the background of her mind. This last week had been a whirlwind. She could hardly believe that she and Jeremy had been married a week ago today. When she'd met him, he had not measured up to her expectations. Even though she had come west as a mail order bride, she wasn't happy that her future seemed all mapped out. She had wanted freedom to do as she pleased. Run her own business without anyone having a right to interfere.

But as the week unfolded, she had found in her husband a man who was kind and considerate. He read his Bible and prayed. His reputation in town was solid.

Someone you picked for me, Lord. Thank you.

Jeremy squeezed her hand. What did Preacher Sutton say? Something about the worth of a virtuous wife being above rubies. She turned a wondering eye on her husband. Did he think that of her?

Then the preacher read out of Proverbs that the heart of a husband can safely trust her. Jeremy smiled, but he kept his eyes forward. Still, he squeezed her hand. She squeezed back, and his smile widened.

Marianne turned her eyes forward too. She had never really thought about this passage of Scripture. But she knew she wanted to be like that woman from Proverbs.

Just as Preacher Sutton proclaimed a benediction, ending the service, a man hurried into the church with a note for Sheriff Goodwin. He rose and followed the messenger out of the church.

Marianne felt Jeremy stiffen beside her, then relax.

"Do you think that had something to do with Mr. Kircher?" Marianne whispered.

"No, of course not. Our jail is secure, and a guard was set to watch him. He's not going anywhere." Jeremy's voice was firm.

But Marianne heard echoes of *don't worry* from earlier in the week and shuddered. Jeremy slipped his arm around her as they stood to sing a final hymn.

After the service, the brides gathered around Marianne and Ella.

"I heard the deputy is worried about an outlaw. Did he really take you target shooting, Ella?"

"Marianne, it was terrible enough to see how badly damaged your husband's shop was, but you must have been terrified by the attack by that man yesterday. How are you doing?"

Val strode up and laid a hand on Marianne's and Ella's shoulders. "I deeply regret that I have brought either of you into danger. I'm praying that this will be the last of the ill will that any of us have to endure." She sent a probing look to Elinore as well.

"Thank you, Val."

"We'll be praying for one another, right?"

"Yes, and for your bakery aspirations, Clara," Cornelia, another bride, agreed.

Clara rewarded her with a gratified smile.

"Will you be all right, Marianne?" Val's concerned gaze now shifted to her.

"Yes, of course I will. Thank you, Val." Marianne looked for Jeremy, and he met her gaze from across the room, where he stood, staff in hand, talking to the McNeils. She shifted her gaze back to Val, then around at the brides. She loved these women who had become like family to her.

Her eyes strayed again to her husband. Her loyalty was for Jeremy. And it surprised her how much it mattered that she should guard his heart.

Thank you again for guiding me to Jeremy. He's a good man, Lord. One who wants to serve You.

* * *

Jeremy held the reins to guide the horse and wagon past the logging camp. He followed McNeils out of town for a short distance before he turned off the main road. Thad had taken Marianne's chairs with them, and everyone waved as they parted ways.

Jeremy shook off his unease. Kircher was in jail. They were perfectly safe. They couldn't live their lives in fear. Today he determined to enjoy the afternoon with his bride as they scouted for a Christmas tree. He wanted Marianne to see more than the shops and street in town. He loved this area and wanted her to love it too.

Logs bobbed in the water as they lumbered alongside the lake. Low, gray clouds obscured the mountains in the distance and drifted laterally on the surface. A hush permeated the afternoon.

Jeremy halted the horse so they could look over the lake.

"Have you yet heard the legend connected with the island out there in the middle of the lake?"

She leaned forward to peer around him and shook her head. "I can barely see it with the clouds and darkness. Is it a spooky legend?"

"Of course. You see it goes like this. It's a belief that giants once lived in this land."

"Ooooh, giants?"

"Yes. Giants. A giant couple lived with their two giant sons above the North Cliffs way at the far end of the lake."

"I can't see them."

"No, not today. Well, Giant Mother admonished her giant sons not to play at the base of the mountain because a monster had a lair in a cave. It was just too dangerous." Jeremy shook his head.

"And did they?"

"Of course they did. They were boys. Boys must explore."

"Naturally, they must." Marianne laughed.

"One day they were playing leapfrog or some such game, as giant boys do—"

"Must it be leapfrog?"

"Stop interrupting. They were playing leapfrog and lost track of time."

He paused and crooked an eyebrow at her. But she remained silent.

"The monster saw them and snatched them up with his mighty long claws."

"Oh no!" Marianne took a hand out of her muff and put it to her forehead. "Tell me they were rescued."

"Alas, no, my dear. Their screams alerted Giant Mother and Giant Father, and they did all they could.

Giant Father threw a huge boulder down at the cave, hoping to free his giant sons, but they were too far underground."

"Jeremy! This is a sad story."

He reached for her hand and stroked it. "I know. Giant Mother sat beside the crater that the boulder made and cried and cried. Her tears filled the space and created the lake in the shape of a rose. An island grew above the very spot where the monster's lair was."

"I'm so sad for Giant Mother and Giant Father."

"Yes. Upon stormy occasions, people say the monster's tail is thrashing beneath the island, where he is trapped."

She leaned and squinted, trying to see the shadowy island. Jeremy took the opportunity to wrap his arms around her and kiss her forehead. Well, as much as he could under that pesky hat she wore.

"We should move on." He searched the sky, reluctant to let her go, and picked up the reins.

"I have not been on this side of town," Marianne commented as she looked around. The trail climbed slightly, and the horse trod easily on the crunchy snow. "It looks like quite a bit of snow has melted in places."

He shifted his ever-painful knees. He still felt Marianne's touch from last night on them.

"Yep. We haven't seen snow since Thursday, so we shouldn't have too much trouble getting a couple small trees today. You warm enough?" He guided the horse carefully into one of the sparse forested areas near town.

"Yes." She pulled her muff closer. "Do you think it will snow before we go back to town?" She scrutinized the sky.

He glanced up. "I think we'll be fine. In fact, this is a good place to stop." He pulled the brake and carefully let himself down from the wagon seat. He huffed as he considered how to be the gentleman and help his lady out of the wagon.

Marianne scooted over, dropped her muff, and began to climb down. He moved close behind her and put his hands on her waist to ease the drop. She turned around, and they stared at each other. Their breath mingled in little puffs of steam. He knew the moment she surrendered, and he pulled her close.

This kiss was not the soft, gentle caress of the night before. He couldn't help it. She yielded under the crush of this kiss and gave back. He hauled her closer, and her arms draped around him. He kissed her until his head swam.

The horse snorted.

She laughed. After pulling himself together, he laughed with her.

"I'm not cold anymore," she murmured.

He grinned. Just one more quick kiss.

He released her and reached into the wagon bed for his double-bit felling axe. He held it up, remembering how proud he was to purchase this. He hadn't used it now in a couple of years. Once it had been his pride and joy. Now it just brought back what happened that awful day.

Today he would make new memories with it. He composed his features, swung around, and held out a hand to Marianne.

She hesitated. "Would you like me to bring your walking stick?"

He met her eyes. "Yes. I suppose it had better come." Now it was his turn to hesitate. "I want to swing your hand as we walk."

* * *

"How about this one?" Jeremy stood beside a small tree that stood as high as his shoulders.

Marianne leaned her elbow on his walking stick and pursed her lips. She cocked her head to one side and then the other.

Jeremy shifted on his feet. "Marianne. It doesn't take that long to size up a tree."

"Oh, all right. I suppose that one will do." She grinned and relented. "Jeremy, it's perfect for the sitting room."

He nodded and swung the axe. She gritted her teeth. Would he be all right doing that? She didn't dare ask.

A few swings and the tree fell over.

"You did that so quickly."

He straightened up under her admiration. "It's all in the technique. You study the tree and look for the best places to strike."

"Should we take it back to the wagon before getting the second one?"

He considered her suggestion, looking back toward the wagon and around the area.

"That is probably a good idea." He hefted the tree and faltered.

She handed him his stick and went to the other end of the tree. When he glared, she glared back. She wasn't about to let his pride sink him when she was perfectly capable of helping to drag this tree.

She heard a pecking noise as they delivered the tree and looked around.

"It's a woodpecker. One of the few bird species that stick around when it gets cold. Now and then you might see a squirrel though—they like to stay warm. Rabbits run freely. You might see one of those."

"Okay. I hope I do see a bunny."

He chuckled and she relaxed.

Soon the second tree was in the wagon. Jeremy gave Marianne a boost to the wagon seat and climbed up himself. She made sure his walking stick was in the back. She tugged a basket over the seat and offered him a cup of hot chocolate before pouring one for herself, from a ceramic jug.

Jeremy urged the horse forward.

"Thank you for this lovely afternoon, Jeremy. It's the best day that I can remember in a long time."

* * *

Jeremy sat in his easy chair. He didn't want to admit that his knees had taken a beating and he needed to be off them. But his wife was beginning to read him. When they'd arrived home, he'd set a tree up in her shop by the front window and the other in the sitting room. She then pushed him into his chair and told him to stay put. She had fixed a quick meal and served him in his chair. He could get used to this. He wished he didn't have to.

He grinned as he sipped his coffee and watched as she popped corn on the cookstove. She had brought ribbons and objects to cover with fabric to decorate the trees. She expected him to string the popcorn for garlands. Who would have thought that he would do such a thing? He sure wouldn't tell anyone.

Marianne carried the bowl of popcorn to the table by his chair, accompanied by several threaded needles.

He plunged his hand into the popcorn and shoved it into his mouth, holding her glance.

"You don't need to look so gleeful. I popped extra, you know. I thought you'd eat it."

He laughed through his mouthful at her school-marmish attitude.

She had just sat down with her ribbons when a knock came at the back door. They looked at each other. No one had come to the back sitting room door all week.

Marianne rose to answer it.

"Stop. I will answer it." He grabbed his stick and pulled himself to his feet. She followed close behind him. He wished she would stay back but saved his breath.

Sheriff Goodwin stood there, his hat shoved back and hands in his coat pocket.

"I'm sorry to bother you this evening, but I need to let you know that Ambrose Kircher escaped from jail today. We are searching for him. Keep an eye out and be careful."

Twelve

J eremy set down his carving tools and stood to stretch. It seemed like he had been bent over this figure for hours. But it had to be right. It was the Christ child, after all. He limped around his work-table, trying to work the kinks out of his knees. He lowered, then stood up again, bending his knees back and forth, one at a time. At least he could move around—that was better than it used to be. He wished the pain would go away but was resigned to it being present in his life forever.

What was that the apostle Paul said? Something about praying three times for God to remove a physical pain from him. And God's answer was that His grace was enough. Paul would live with the pain reminder that God was with him.

Jeremy didn't feel strong enough to live with such a painful reminder. Yet he had no choice. This was his lot. He had to learn to live with it. Like Paul.

He looked around the shop. The window was still boarded up. The new window would arrive after Christmas. It sure made the place look dingy, even though he kept it tidy. How could a person do their work if they couldn't find their tools in the right places?

This was his calling. Every time a customer picked up an item that Jeremy had created, satisfaction sat on his shoulders. He felt it in the smiles of his purchasers. Most of the dolls and horse figures he had crafted had not been touched by Kircher's rage last week. That would make Prentiss happy at the mercantile. He had to get them over there. The small things had been put away. Some homes would see children's faces light up. Jeremy smiled to imagine it.

He breathed deeply of the aromas of the shop. Marianne's mock orange blossom perfume mingled with the smells of wood, paint, turpentine, and furniture polish. He would appreciate whiffs of her perfume every day. Come spring he might have to transplant a mock orange bush from the forest to his back yard.

Jeremy studied the form of the Christ child on his bench. It should lay in its container perfectly.

He picked up the Christ figure and placed it in the manger in a back corner of the shop, behind his tool shelves, grateful he had placed the figures back here, since they had escaped destruction. He pulled up a stool and sat down, one arm resting on the length of the manger.

He regarded the Christ figure. He lowered his head. The sounds of Marianne moving around in her shop comforted him. She was safe.

He didn't think Kircher would enter the millinery again. And with the snow coming down so heavily, he doubted the man would even be outside. At least, not in town. Where would he go? If he were sighted, he would be back in jail faster than he could lift a bottle to his mouth.

Thank you, Lord, for bringing Amos here to warn us last night.

A warning was a good thing. It meant Jeremy could plan and prepare. He had to protect his wife. They had a future to build. He wanted that future more than anything.

He felt again the press of her sweet lips. His own tingled in anticipation.

He groaned. He just didn't know what Ambrose Kircher would do. There had been a time they had been friends. They had looked out for each other and for Aichen Kircher. They worked together, pulled saws together. Even rolled on logs in the water on Sundays together. How had things come to this?

His wife and even his own life in danger because his friend had become his enemy. Those words kept rolling around in his mind. A mantra with no answer. Would he always be looking over his shoulder? And what if he couldn't defend Marianne or himself because of his limitations?

He gripped the manger with one hand and pounded a knee with the other. Less than a man. That was who he was now. Having to walk around with a crutch like an old man. How could he protect a family like this?

God, there is nowhere to turn but you. Please protect Marianne if I cannot. She doesn't deserve to suffer. Are You there?

* * *

Marianne jabbed and tugged pieces of holly onto Mrs. Beck's new hat. So many issues for her friends running through her mind. Wild Rose Ridge was not the quiet little town they had all believed they would settle in.

She jabbed again as she thought of how Mrs. Beck had snubbed Elinore and her mother-in-law. How rude.

Then yesterday someone came into her shop to inform her that her friend Elizabeth Ann had been trapped all Saturday night with a miner after a cave in. Marianne set the hat in her lap for a moment. Thank God they had been found in time. And now Elizabeth Ann was to marry the miner she'd been trapped with. He wasn't the groom she came to marry.

Marianne shook her head. She hoped her friend would find a happy union.

She sighed and set the hat on a block to step back and study it. She folded her arms across her chest and propped a finger under her chin; she considered her client and this new design. She hoped Mrs. Beck would like it. Considering that lady liked oversized creations on her head, this hat was much less pretentious. One side dipped lower than the other. Marianne hoped that this headpiece would stay on top of Mrs. Beck's head as well as satisfying her desire for opulence in her appearance.

Red berries drooped down that side and contrasted with the black form. Red and white ribbons sashed around the crown with sprigs of holly tucked in. Green bows provided symmetry on the higher side opposite the berries. Black netting stretched across the front. The hat was ready for Mrs. Beck to wear to her Christmas events.

The Christmas Eve dance was only two days away. How did the time fly so fast?

Her original wedding had been planned for that night. Now she would be attending several weddings of her fellow brides after the dance.

Marianne had brought a gown with her for a Christmas occasion. She would not be wearing the same gown she had worn for her wedding last week. This one was simpler, yet elegant. Midnight-blue brocade with black lace for trim across the décolleté, down the skirt, and at the back for the bustle. Long black lace gloves and a matching cape would complete the outfit. When she had packed it weeks ago, Christmas had been a long way off. And now the Christmas Eve dance was two days away. Would Jeremy admire her in it? Maybe more than admire her? Maybe turn a corner in their marriage.

Where did that thought come from? She was perfectly happy with the way things were. Suddenly she was back in the woods with prickles chasing through her as Jeremy kissed her. He wasn't the only one with wobbly knees either. How forest, cold air, and even gray sky had disappeared in the bliss of his arms around her.

And his lips on hers.

She wrenched her mind from the woods.

Her fingers on her mouth, she turned from Mrs. Beck's hat and paced across the bare space from the glass counter to gaze out the window at the falling snow. It had snowed all day yesterday and still snowed today. Foot traffic was light then and today. Few people were out in the street.

She returned to the counter, set Mrs. Beck's hat aside, and entered her workspace. She needed to have a hat ready for Miss Luisa, Ella's protégé. She rummaged through her supplies. She thought she surely should have the ribbon she needed. But no. None of her bins had what she wanted. This hat had to be perfect to help transform a little hooligan into a young lady.

There was no help for it. She would have to run across the street to the mercantile. She grabbed her reticule and cloak and set a warm hat on her head. She didn't particularly care to have a wet head the rest of the afternoon.

She paused and looked out the window again. The store was just a few feet away. She didn't see anyone out there. Ambrose Kircher had probably left the area after his Sunday jailbreak. She wouldn't be gone long.

"Jeremy," she called, "I'm stepping out to the mercantile for a few minutes. I won't be gone long. Not to worry."

She left their shops and carefully made her way on the ice and into the snow. Abruptly, she was grabbed by the arm and yanked farther into the street.

* * *

No!

Jeremy heard her call. "No, wait. Don't go alone." He jumped up and grabbed his stick and limped to the door.

When he heard her scream, he dropped the stick and ran. His knees shifted from throbbing to smarting, but he ignored them.

"About time you showed up, Stafford," Ambrose Kircher shouted. He gripped Marianne's arm. She twisted and turned, but his grasp held firm.

"Let her go." Jeremy stuttered to a halt. "She's done nothing to hurt you."

"I've got her for Aichen." Marianne tried to wrench herself free again, and Kircher slapped her. "I told you to calm down. Aichen will treat you right."

Jeremy took another step closer. He wanted to throw himself at Kircher and beat the tar out of him for striking Marianne. His face must have shown his rage, because she stared at him helplessly. Frustration boiled through him. The first opportunity he got, he would take Kircher down.

"Don't even think it, Stafford. I got this bride for Aichen. You don't deserve to be here."

Same old refrain that Kircher had spewed before, and Jeremy was sick of hearing it. "What about you, Kircher? Why didn't you rush in to save your brother?"

"My brother is fine. Stay clear, Stafford. You're a nothing, Stafford. I've got a gun, and I'm gonna get you after I take care of her. Gonna make sure Aichen gets her. Gonna right the wrong." He held up the weapon, and it wavered as he kept his grip on Marianne.

Jeremy fixed his eyes on the pistol even as he registered a group of men gathering quietly.

"The only wrong is you abducting an innocent woman, Kircher. Let her go."

"Not a chance. I told you—I'm taking her to Aichen, where she belongs. You're done, Stafford." Kircher strode forward, dragging Marianne behind him, prodding her with the gun.

Jeremy followed. Even with his limp, he was closer, thanks to Marianne's squirming efforts. Out of the corner of his eye, he saw the sheriff and a couple of temporary deputies slide around the back of his building and the bathhouse across the street. After that, the fields would offer no impediment to Kircher's progress out of town.

But neither would it hide him from pursuers.

The snow fell more heavily, and large flakes worked to obscure visibility. Jeremy pushed down the panic that tried to freeze him. He had to reach Marianne. He had to free her.

Kircher hauled her farther down the street toward the open fields. "C'mon, Aichen's waiting. We have to get to him."

"No. I don't know Aichen," Marianne cried, using her free hand to punch at Kircher. He tried to restrain her free arm and missed.

As he missed, he slid on the ice and fell, and the gun discharged into the air. Marianne went down with him. Between the snow and her billowing skirts, Jeremy could not see her for a moment.

He sprinted, and his legs slipped out from under him. He went down with an explosion of pain and saw lightning before blackness.

* * *

Surprised, Marianne lay motionless for a moment. What had happened? Was she shot? She flexed her arms and toes, then sat up.

Ambrose Kircher did not move. The sheriff and his men surrounded them.

"Jeremy?" She scanned each figure in the blinding snow. Was he there? Was he shot?

"He's with Patrick Schulte. Doc Paine will be here as soon as we can fetch him from the Cameron ranch. Patrick is our veterinarian and fills in for Doc Paine. Jeremy is in good hands. Prentiss, take her over to him." Sheriff Goodwin helped her to her feet. "Careful now. You've already had one fall, and it's slick."

"Thank you, Sheriff."

Mr. Prentiss, the storekeeper, took her lightly by the elbow to steer her in the right direction.

She saw Jeremy on the ground and rushed toward him.

"Slow and careful if you plan to get to him," the man escorting her said calmly.

When she finally stood beside Jeremy's prone form, she dropped. She didn't know if the wetness on her cheeks was due to the snow or her tears. She didn't care. Jeremy had come after her to his own hurt. She didn't see any blood, and instead saw stars for a moment in her relief.

"Doc?"

"He'll be fine." Patrick Schulte ran his hands over Jeremy. "Let's get him inside. Mrs. Stafford, can you make him comfortable? It looks like his legs took the brunt. Thanks, Henry, for reaching him before his head hit the ground with full impact."

A law volunteer nodded solemnly. "He threw out his hands, and that seems to have protected his head somewhat. I need to see to the other man, and I will be back after that."

Marianne gulped her tears back and straightened. Arms pulled her to her feet, and then Jeremy was lifted. He groaned as they boosted his legs, and she swallowed. He wouldn't be in this shape if she had not ventured out on her own, knowing Kircher had escaped the jail.

She led the way inside to his bed, where they laid him. As they pulled off his muddy boots and worked to remove his suspenders and wet pants, she left the room.

In the kitchen, Marianne tossed her muddy cloak onto a chair. Her reticule had wrapped around her wrist, and she untwisted the strings and tossed it onto the cloak. She put a hand to her head instinctively, but her hat had disappeared in the fray.

She filled a bowl with warm water from the reservoir on the side of the cookstove and snatched a towel on her way back to the bedroom.

Her face warm, she hoped they had been able to get Jeremy into bed. His pants and suspenders lay in a heap on the floor above his boots. She let a sigh of relief escape her.

"Can you manage now, ma'am?"

She faced the two men who had carried her husband into the safe warmth.

"Thank you so much, Mr. Prentiss and Mr. Blevins. I'm so grateful. Yes, I can manage. Please tell the doctor to come straight in when he arrives here."

"Surely will, ma'am." Both men dipped their heads and left.

Marianne faced her husband and breathed deeply. She loved him. He had sacrificed himself for her today, coming after her despite the threat of his own injuries. It was her own fault he lay still now.

She sat on the bed and stripped away the wet shirt. He was so cold. He had run into a snowfall after her without a coat. Her heart pounded as she dried him and slipped on his nightshirt. She held him close, trying to warm him with her own body, as she smoothed the dry shirt across his back. She hesitated as she studied his face so close to hers. Gentle in repose. She softly kissed his temple and laid him down.

His eyes were open and stared into hers.

"Oh. H . . . how do you feel?"

"Like a tree fell on my knees," he croaked.

"Oh, Jeremy." Her throat filled, and she couldn't speak further.

"I'm sorry I couldn't rescue you."

Her heart broke.

Thirteen

Jeremy opened his eyes. He blinked, shut them, and tried again. The room was fuzzy. His mouth felt full of cotton. At least his head didn't hurt. It was probably the only part of his body that didn't.

His vision cleared a bit, and he looked around. He was in his own room. But why was there a curtain hanging in the middle?

Wait, he knew.

He felt like he did while he recuperated at McNeils'. But that was then. This was now. And now it meant that he had a bride on the other side of the curtain.

He had to protect her.

He moved his legs and groaned.

The curtain squeaked as a portion of it folded upon itself.

"Jeremy?"

He turned his head on the pillow and met concerned, yet sleepy, blue eyes fixed on him. She leaned on one elbow. He struggled to find a smile. Even in the throes of his awakening pain, he was aware of her. His sweet, adorable wife.

"Yes?" He could barely push the word out.

She disappeared. But before he could be disappointed, she rounded the end of the curtain and fiddled with something on his night table.

"Here." She held a spoon. "Doc Paine left this for you. To ease your discomfort and help you sleep."

He eyed it. Laudanum. Yes, he recognized that. He looked toward the wall. Not again. He was past that point. He clamped his mouth and shut his eyes.

"Jeremy, please, it will help speed recovery." She sat on the bed, the spoon still in her hand.

He turned toward her, and the softness in her eyes held his gaze. Her ruffled nightgown and braided hair distracted him. And his knees throbbed through his whole body. He didn't want to be this weak man in her presence. He didn't want her to nurse him. He didn't want to need nursing.

"If you won't take it from me, then I will go get Thad. He slept in the sitting room last night. Henry Blevins went after him when we got you to bed, to come help us."

"I will take it. But let me see Thad first." He steeled himself from the hurt in her eyes, and she started to rise. He closed a hand around her arm. She spilled the spoonful of medicine, and he eyed it with satisfaction. He hated what laudanum did, but he hated the pain it combated more.

"Marianne. Thank you. Your presence is sweet. But Thad knows what I need for now." He let go, and her tremulous attempt at a smile had to be his reward. He was sure his own smile attempt looked more like a grimace.

"I'll get him and see about breakfast."

He let her go this time. She set the spoon next to the bottle on his table, picked up a towel, and wiped up the liquid that had already soaked into the sheet. She picked up a robe and tied it around her waist and gave him a last look before leaving the room.

Jeremy shut his eyes. The events of yesterday came back to him and played in his mind. He could only hope he had not injured his knees further.

"Well, my fine man, so your bride tells me you are awake, in pain, and refusing the medicine," Thad clomped in the door and leaned against the wall, arms crossed. He studied Jeremy with a practiced eye.

Jeremy forced himself not to squirm under what he had come to think of as the Dr. Thad look. "You missed your calling."

Amusement lit Thad's face. "So you've said a number of times. I suppose you are not as bad off as I feared if you can back talk me already. Why won't you take the laudanum?"

Jeremy eyed Thad and twisted his lips.

"Oh, that." Thad laughed.

After Jeremy was comfortable again and Thad took the pot outside, Marianne came in with a mug of coffee and warm bread and butter. She set it down, and before she could move aside, Jeremy grabbed her hand and placed a kiss on it.

"Thank you, my bride."

She smiled genuinely this time. "I hope you'll take your medicine again soon. The doctor said a day of rest and sleep will help to restore you."

"I will be up tomorrow." He was determined. Even if he had to ask Thad to fetch the despised crutches from his workroom. He would be up. But for now, he knew better. Bless his friend Thad.

Marianne slipped behind her curtain to dress, then she left the room.

Thad returned with the chamber pot.

"Kircher?"

Thad shoved the pot under the bed and sat down. "Sheriff Goodwin sent Blevins over this morning to let us know that Kircher is still unconscious. In light of his rantings and threats yesterday, which the whole town heard, Doc Paine wants to send him to the mental hospital at Fort Steilacoom."

"That's across the territory to the west, isn't it?"

"Yes. I think the doc is getting paperwork filled out today so Kircher can be moved as quickly as possible."

Jeremy fell silent. His relief at Kircher's leaving the area overlaid his anger at the man. Ambrose Kircher had done no lasting harm. He had nothing to do with the accident that mangled Jeremy's knees. His sin had been to pin blame for his brother's death on Jeremy.

Before Jeremy could move forward, he had to deal with his forgiveness of Kircher.

Help me, Lord, to let go of this whole business into Your hands along with Ambrose Kircher. I guess a man can be weak in more ways than one. Give me strength, Lord. Give me strength to follow You.

* * *

Today, while Thad was here, Marianne would scoot to the mercantile for the supplies she needed. The ones she couldn't get yesterday.

Snow fell intermittently through the day. Marianne took special care in her errand, mindful of the ice underneath. Today she had been more attentive to everyone around her. It felt strange to be doing the very same errand today that had caused so much trouble yesterday. But now that Ambrose Kircher would be taken away, she had no reason to fear.

Nor would she live a life of fear. Caution, yes, that might be necessary at times. But not fear. The Good Book stated that God gave a sound mind and power to live in that sound mind, and fear had no place in her thoughts. Therefore, she would act on that sound-mind power and not allow fright to stop her.

She crossed the street. She bought ribbons, lace, and holly, then crossed the street again to come home. All the while she looked around her.

Would she tell Jeremy she'd gone? She bit her lip as she worked the holly into the crown of the straw hat and matched ribbons and lace, for the little girl Ella had taken charge of. Deputy Garrison's daughter. She held the hat out. Red and green streamers flowed from the back. Yes, it was demure and sweet. Just right for a little girl.

No, maybe she wouldn't tell Jeremy.

She set the hat on a block and folded her hands in her lap. Snow still fell, and the gray sky melded into darkness.

Her heart had broken last night right along with Jeremy's broken voice when he'd apologized for not being able to rescue her. Didn't he know he had already rescued her?

No one had ever sacrificed anything for her. Yet Jeremy did.

He had sacrificed injury again to run after her in danger.

He had thoughtfully built a home for her. And a shop to fulfill her wish to be an independent woman. In her business. He wanted a wife. She wanted to be that wife.

When had her heart become involved in this contract marriage? Certainly not at first, when Jeremy had insisted that she marry him because she had signed a contract. She smiled at how she had run to Val O'Malley to fix things the way she wanted. That didn't happen. She was now grateful.

Even while arguing, Jeremy had been polite—icily so. Yet when she saw him the very next day, he'd kissed her hand when they'd married. His eyes had been apologetic yet curiously alight. Not brown eyes to match his brown suit. No, expressive hazel eyes sparkling with green and brown lights in them.

It wasn't independence she needed.

Perhaps true independence lay in becoming dependent.

Marianne was humbled. She hung her head. God had directed her to this place and to the protection of a kind, thoughtful husband. But she had thought she had known better than either of them.

Her God was worthy of her love, devotion, and obedience.

Her husband was a man of integrity and worthy of her respect.

He had won her. How could she show him?

* * *

Jeremy grunted as he struggled with the crutches that Thad had fetched for him. How lucky that they'd been propped up in the corner of the bedroom. He had intended to take them out to the workshop but had forgotten. God's intervention yet again?

"You sure you want to try this today? Doc did tell you to give your knees a rest, you know." Thad stood beside Jeremy at the ready to catch him.

Jeremy sat and panted. He pulled his shirttails down. At least the suspenders held his clothes mostly in place. Thad

had helped him get his pants on. Jeremy would not lay around in his nightshirt.

Sweat popped out on his forehead, and he gritted his teeth for the next try.

"Don't help me. I will get up."

"Yeah, I can see that."

Jeremy gripped the handles of the crutches and hauled himself to his feet. He grinned.

"Victory!"

"Good job, man." Thad crossed his arms and stepped back. "Now what?"

Jeremy dropped to the bed, out of breath. "I'm not ready for Sylvester Sneed's services yet. If he shows up, don't let him in."

Thad guffawed. "Don't want to listen to any slogans from our local undertaker, eh?"

Jeremy glowered at his friend and laid the props on the floor to slide them under the bed. They clanked with the chamber pot.

"Here, let me arrange those so you can reach them easily." Thad maneuvered them and stood again. "It's getting dark, Jer. I need to head home."

Jeremy held out his hand and Thad shook it.

"Thanks for coming in. I appreciate it. I promise to take care. But I have to be up tomorrow. It's Christmas Eve, and I must take my bride to the dance."

"Uh-huh. Some figure you will cut on the dance floor."

Jeremy agreed. "You know I won't attempt anything like that. But this is a big event, and I don't want her to miss it. Be safe heading home."

Thad nodded and left.

Jeremy leaned over and reached for the crutches. He

heard Thad's and Marianne's voices in the distance. She would probably plan to fix supper for them. He might have a few minutes to practice getting up and down on these support sticks before she had it ready.

Who knew how much energy could be sapped out of a body in a day?

He heard a gasp behind him and twisted to see her. The crutches wobbled, and Marianne rushed to brace him. He let go of the props to grab her, and they fell onto the bed together. He winced as pain shot through his knees but forgot the hurt as he stared into her luminous blue eyes so close to his. Neither of them moved.

Her curves fit perfectly in all the right places. Jeremy did what any man would do. Wrapping his arms tightly around her, he kissed her.

* * *

Jeremy's fingers running through her hair penetrated Marianne's foggy brain. His embrace had relaxed, but she didn't want to move. His lips pressed hers again and again until she couldn't breathe.

He shifted beneath her, and she abruptly sat up and shoved her hair away from her heated face. When had her hair fallen out of its neat bun?

Jeremy gently tugged her toward him, but she stood up. He grunted and sat up with his hands on the bed on either side of him.

"Your knees." She gulped.

"What about my knees?" He frowned.

She didn't answer but carefully picked up his legs and moved them onto the bed.

"Marianne."

She ignored his grumpy voice and sat on the bed again. "I suppose you will refuse any laudanum?"

"You suppose right. I'd like to return to what we were doing."

She smiled, and he rewarded her with his grin. This time when he tugged, she lay down next to him. He scooted closer to the wall to give her room.

"You're sweet, my love. And tender. And I'm grateful we are both here together."

"Jeremy, I—"

He silenced her with another kiss. Oh my. Was this a swoon? She could stay here forever.

"Jeremy." He trailed kisses along her neck, and she panted. "We . . . we have to talk."

He groaned but leaned back.

"Okay. Talk." He sounded out of breath too. That pleased her.

"I am grateful that we are together here too." She whispered, barely able to get words out. She cleared her throat. "I-I was afraid I might lose you. And I knew then that I-I just couldn't lose you. I-I love you, Jeremy." She stared at him. She'd said it.

His hazel eyes softened, green melding into brown. "I've known that I love you for a long time, sweetheart. I couldn't help falling in love with you. I think the first time I saw you."

"You couldn't have. I was so mean to you."

"That you were." He chuckled. "But I wasn't exactly the gentleman to you either. Insisting on marriage because you signed a contract wasn't very romantic."

She giggled. "I was so mad. I went to Val to see what

could be done. Nothing, it seemed. Unless I ran home, which I could not do."

"I'm sorry your family forced you out."

"It brought me here. To you." She leaned over to kiss him this time. But when he reached for her again, she backed away. She wasn't done talking.

Jeremy seemed to realize that kissing would have to wait. He settled his back against the wall and tipped his head to regard her.

They sat silent for a moment. Then he took a deep breath.

"I wanted a legacy, Marianne. It was so important that I not just pass through this life without being remembered for something. But now that isn't what is important to me. I just want to love you and trust God for our lives together.

"I learned this week that only God can truly guard us," he said. "I wanted to be the one to guard you. But right after I prayed that, Ambrose showed up again and I couldn't get to you. I've struggled a long time wanting to be the strong man you can count on."

She felt as if Jeremy had handed her his treasures. He had laid his soul bare. She was on holy ground now, and her heart expanded to fill her own soul. Tears stung her eyes at the beauty of it. She ran her hand tenderly down the side of his face. He leaned into it.

"You are that man, Jeremy."

His eyes flew open and burned into hers.

"I know now that God is worthy of my faith, love, and my obedience. He sent me to a man of integrity, who is worthy of my respect."

He lifted her hand to his lips, his eyes never leaving hers. "I promise, as it is always in my power, to be the husband you deserve. To love you, care for you, and to be present with you in all the ways that I can. I love you, my sweet Marianne."

"I promise to honor you as best I can. And let God show me how. I love you too, Jeremy, my kind, strong husband."

Epilogue

December 26, 1885
     Wild Rose Ridge
     Dearest Mama,

Merry Christmas and Happy New Year to you and everyone there. I miss all of you. I'm sure you will be glad to know that I am at home here. Christmas was lovely and exciting, and I look forward to a joyful new year too.

This might be a longer than my usual epistle.

Everything is wonderful. I have been married now for two amazing weeks. I married Jeremy Stafford, the man I told you about in my last missive. He's everything I could hope for, Mama. You would like him. Maybe one day we can travel to see you.

Jeremy is not tall. We are of a height, but he is a giant in my eyes. And a hero in the community. He was once a logger and injured his knees in an accident while trying to save the life of another man. We both know that God orders all the affairs of men, and we are content.

I think I mentioned before that Jeremy owns a carpentry business and does quite well. He is an artist woodcarver and carved a Christ child figure and a manger. We will work together to round out a Nativity setting. I can't decide whether I want it in my shop or in our private quarters.

You will be happy to know that the shop he built for my millinery business is doing well too. We are in the process of decorating it, and I have fashioned and sold hats to several ladies already. I love that we work side by side (sort of, in the same building) and that he encourages my efforts.

Did I say that you would like him, Mama?

I know you will be interested in how all the brides have managed. Jeremy and I wed the day after my arrival. We shared our wedding with my friend Elinore and her husband, Robert Cameron. Elinore left town to settle in with Mr. Cameron and his mother. I see them now and then. Elinore has invited me to tea at her home, but we haven't been able to set a time yet. Her husband has been ill. But I'm sure, once he is recovered and Christmas is over, we will be able to do so.

You would like our Busy Bees. These are the society ladies of Wild Rose Ridge who contracted with Sisters Mail Order Bride Company to bring us from Chicago. The ladies have been active in making sure we found our grooms and places in society. All the brides are married now. Aside from Elinore and myself, a huge wedding ceremony was hosted by the Bees after a Christmas Eve dance. Preacher Sutton married everyone off at the same time. It was a joyous occasion. And our own Val O'Malley agreed to marry Preacher Sutton the same night. Though they will have to wait for the itinerant preacher to come. After all, Preacher Sutton can't perform his own ceremony. Still, it was all so romantic.

I was able to wear that midnight-blue and black lace ball gown that you wanted me to bring. Jeremy looked so dapper in his evening attire. We couldn't dance, but we sat and held hands as everyone danced in front of us. Although I was asked a few times and Jeremy urged me to dance. But mostly I just wanted to sit with him.

The town is growing. I think Wild Rose Ridge needed us. We have brought many skills to the town. Sewing and tailoring, a bakery, millinery, schooling, and of course, homemaking.

I need to close this letter for now. I look forward to receiving a communication from you soon. Please give my regards to everyone.

Love from your daughter,
Marianne Stafford

A Note to My Readers

When I began my research for this project, I was surprised to learn the important role that mail order marriages played in the building of the United States as a country. With the Civil War leaving a dearth of men in the East and the lack of women in the West, a whole industry grew up.

Much like the modern online dating, these were men and women who put ads in papers and magazines nation-wide. They usually sent photos and wrote letters to each other before entering into any contracts.

Most of the marriages started out looking for companionship, legacy, and survival. Not all prospective couples married, and some marriages did not last long. But others lasted for fifty years and more. Friendship was bedrock. Love was defined more on the biblical commitments of love rather than romantic expectations. It took sturdy spirits and sturdy hearts to overcome the obstacles they had to endure in a time when making a living took determination.

I admire them. They forged an inheritance for us who came after them.

Acknowledgments

Thank you to my My Book Therapy Huddle buddies: Kit Morgan, Dalyn Weller, Mary Albers Felkins, Kathy Geary Anderson, Alyssa Schwarz, and Christine Sterling. You bless me so much, and I treasure our friendship. We are on an adventure together. Bless you gals!

Thank you to Amy Petrowich, who keeps our stories on track with the others.

Thank you to Dori Harrell, Breakout Editing. She has taught me a lot in how to use words well, and how to use Microsoft Word manuscript formatting tools to make a good, clean copy. She said editors like that. She polishes up my opuses so they shine. I'm grateful.

Thank you to Heather J. Wilbur for creating such fun maps. Even to this latest historical map of our fictional town. She has made all of our Wild Rose Ridge maps, and they are all beautiful and easy to read. So much better than the scribbles I gave her to work with.

Scribettes, my local writers group, encourages me immensely. I am thankful for the years we have been together, writing our prompts, praying for and blessing each other. Gail Justesen, Dianna Brumfield, Joann Husted, Diana Schepens, Karen Janish, Diane Morissette, Karena Krull, Melissa McConnell, Rose Black, and Katherine Houston. You are all the best!

About Linda Jo Reed

Writing has been a lifelong dream for me. I wrote my first novel in the fifth grade. Thank goodness it disappeared, but it left a mark. I discovered that there is a place for making things up. But life happened.

Since I retired a few years ago, my new career is now a reality. I write a weekly blog at www.lindajoreed.com. I have published three inspirational nonfiction books because it's most important to point the way to our Lord and Savior, Jesus Christ. Several articles and short stories have been published in anthologies. Fiction is just fun and gives plenty of "scope for imagination," as Lucy Montgomery's Anne Shirley would put it.

I live in the beautiful Pacific Northwest, where the mountains reach to God and the skies are blue and gold tinged in the summer. Winter is another story. My nine grandsons are my baseball team, and I have two elderly kitties to love.

About Wild Rose Ridge Authors

The Wild Rose Ridge authors are a small encouragement group (Huddle) of Christian writers. We were formed through a larger organization, My Book Therapy and Novel Academy. Founded by Susan May Warren, the academy teaches writing and marketing and has built a network of Huddles to encourage writers to move forward.

Our Huddle envisioned this novella series during a brainstorming session. Lake Chelan, Washington, serves as the inspiration for our fictional town, lake, and area of Wild Rose Ridge. Though we live in several states, each year we gather in Chelan to retreat. We plan our stories, drink coffee (we're in Washington State, the coffee capital of the world!) and wine, eat charcuterie, and play.

With this Mail Order Bride Christmas series, as a team we enter a new genre for us. We have all enjoyed our journey into the past, where manners, lifestyle, and so much more laid a foundation for who we are today. We hope you have enjoyed these stories of Wild Rose Ridge in the past as much as we have in bringing them to you.

If you have liked them, we invite you to share reviews

on Amazon, Goodreads, or any place else you might like to share how these stories impacted your life.

Check out our page on Facebook: (11) Wild Rose Ridge Readers 🛡 | Facebook

We'd love to know what you enjoyed about your visits to Wild Rose Ridge.

Find out more about the authors and the series here:

Kit Morgan https://www.authorkitmorgan.com/

Linda Jo Reed https://lindajoreed.com/

Mary Albers Felkins https://www.maryfelkins.com/

Kathy Geary Anderson https://www.facebook.com/KathyGearyAndersonAuthor/

Dalyn Weller https://dalynweller.wordpress.com/

Alyssa Schwarz https://www.authoralyssaschwarz.com/

Christine Sterling https://christinesterlingauthor.com

WILD ROSE RIDGE HISTORICALS

Don't miss the other mail-order-brides'
stories this Christmas!

KIT MORGAN

MARY A. FELKINS

KATHY GEARY ANDERSON

CHRISTINE STERLING

ALYSSA SCHWARZ

LINDA JO REED

DALYN WELLER

All books will be
available in
Kindle Unlimited
this Christmas
season

www.ingramcontent.com/pod-product-compliance
Lightning Source LLC
Chambersburg PA
CBHW021046130626
46552CB00005B/2037